MW00781136

CREMAS, CHRISTMAS COOKIES, AND CROOKS

A Cape Bay Cafe Mystery Book 6

HARPER LIN

This is a work of fiction. Names, characters, organizations, places, events, and incidents are either products of the author's imagination or are used fictitiously.

Cremas, Christmas Cookies, and Crooks

Copyright © 2017 by Harper Lin.

All rights reserved.

No part of this book may be reproduced, or stored in a retrieval system, or transmitted in any form or by any means, electronic, mechanical, photocopying, recording, or otherwise, without express written permission of the author.

ISBN-13: 978-1987859485

ISBN-10: 1987859480

www.harperlin.com

Chapter 1

MY HEELS CLIP-CLOPPED on the linoleum floor as I made my way toward the principal's office. I was anxious about being in the hallway in the middle of a school day without a hall pass, but I had no reason to be. It wasn't as though they could suspend me. I'd graduated more than fifteen years ago.

At the office door, I felt the same rush of nervous energy I'd felt when I'd been a student. It didn't matter why I was going to the office—to drop off a stack of freshly printed school newspapers, to pick up the lunch that I'd forgotten, to be taken home early because I was sick—I was always nervous. It was as if I was afraid I'd committed some infraction that they'd decided to only mention if I happened to wander in for something else. Ridiculous, I know.

I swallowed down my nerves and opened the door. The receptionist looked up at me. Smiling, I walked over to her to introduce myself. "Hi, I'm Francesca Amaro—"

"Of course you are, dear! I'd recognize you anywhere! Alice! Come look! Franny Amaro's here!"

If she hadn't been saying my name, I would have been sure she had me confused with someone else.

A woman who I assumed was Alice came from somewhere in the back. "Franny! It's so good to see you! I was so sorry to hear about your mother. How are you doing, dear?"

"Um, I'm fine," I said. "How are you?" I had no idea who these women were, but they sure seemed to know me.

"I don't think she remembers us, Marian," Alice said to the receptionist. "You don't remember us, do you, Franny?"

I searched my brain for these women. Friends of my mother? My grandmother, maybe? They were old enough that they could have been. "Um, no, I'm sorry—"

"I'm Mrs. Bayless, dear," the receptionist said. "And this is Mrs. Crawford."

I looked from one to the other, repeating their names in my head. They sounded familiar. Then I looked at Mrs. Bayless's nameplate in front of her and back at her. I glanced around the room, then at the nameplate, then at her, then at Mrs. Crawford, then back around the room, and suddenly everything clicked. "Oh, Mrs. Bayless! And Mrs. Crawford!" I blushed. "I am so, so sorry!"

"Oh, don't be sorry, dear!" Mrs. Bayless said.

"We're certainly not the spring chickens we used to be!" Mrs. Crawford said.

"No, it's not that," I said. "It's just that I don't think I expected anyone to still be here who was here when I was a student."

"She's just saying that to be nice," Mrs. Crawford stage-whispered to Mrs. Bayless. "She doesn't want to say that she thought we'd be dead by now."

Mrs. Bayless laughed as if it were the funniest thing she'd ever heard.

It wasn't far off from the truth, though. Mrs. Bayless and Mrs. Crawford had been the school secretaries back when I was a student. In my young eyes, they'd been old enough to retire back then, but now I realized that they'd probably only been middle-aged. They didn't actually look all that much different than they had. Their faces had a few more creases, but their hair wasn't even grayer. Hair dye doesn't stop working just because you get older, after all.

"Oh, well, I'm sure you didn't come here just to give us a bit of a laugh, did you, Franny? What can I do for you?" Mrs. Bayless asked, still chuckling a little.

Before I could answer, a door behind Mrs. Bayless opened and a blond teenage boy walked out, followed by a dark-haired man about my age.

"Mrs. Bayless, could you give Brett a note to get back into class? And, Brett, think about what we talked about," he said. He looked at me and nodded before going back into his office and closing the door. The plaque on it read Marcus Varros, and under that, Principal. So at least I knew that my old principal, Mrs. King, was gone.

Mrs. Bayless tapped at her computer then printed something and signed it. She handed the paper to the boy. "I've said this before, but I hope this is the last one of these I have to sign for you, Brett."

The boy looked at her for a second then sighed. "Whatever." He brushed past me and pushed through the door, letting it slam behind him.

"Sorry about that, Franny. Now what can I do for you?" Mrs. Bayless asked.

"I'm here to see Veronica Underwood," I said.

She and Mrs. Crawford exchanged a glance.

"It's about selling some refreshments during the school play."

"Of course, dear. Just sign in right there, and I'll print you out a name tag," Mrs. Bayless said, gesturing at a clipboard on the edge of her desk.

"I understand Veronica is the drama teacher?" I asked as I wrote my information on the form. Something about that look between them made me wonder if there was something they knew that I didn't.

"Yes, dear. She took over from Gwen Blarney this year. But I don't think Gwen was here when you were, was she?"

I thought for a second. "The name doesn't ring a bell." I smiled. "But it took me a minute to recognize your name too."

"I think Ann Crowsdale would have been the drama teacher back when Franny was here," Mrs. Crawford said.

"Ah, yes, that's right," Mrs. Bayless said. "She only teaches English classes now, but she still codirects the play. Are you meeting with her too?"

"I'm not sure. I was just told to ask for Veronica."

"Why am I not surprised?" Mrs. Crawford muttered.

"*Alice*," Mrs. Bayless said sharply then smiled at me. "Veronica has been trying very hard to make her way here, and it's rubbed a few of the staff the wrong way. We get used to things being a certain way, you know. Even when someone has the best of intentions, it can be hard to adapt to new ways."

"I certainly understand," I said and smiled back at her. I was getting the sense that there was more to it than she was telling me, but couldn't imagine that it was anything I needed to get involved with. I was just there to work out the details of selling some coffee and baked goods. I didn't need to concern myself with school politics.

"Here you go, dear," Mrs. Bayless said, handing me the sticky-backed name tag she'd printed out with my name on it. "You don't need us to keep you here, prattling on. Do you remember where the drama room is? It's straight down the hall and down the ramp. You'll go through two sets of double doors and then turn left."

"Thank you very much," I said. "It was nice seeing you again!"

I made my way out of the office and down the

hall. The school had been renovated and added on to at least once since I graduated, but it still felt like the same place. And I didn't know how, but it even smelled the same. Either the old building just had that distinctive odor, or the aroma of teenagers and school lunches hadn't changed much over the years.

The drama room was right where I remembered. The door was open, so I poked my head in. "Veronica?"

"It's Ms. Underwood, and you need to knock."

I was startled for a second but then realized she must have thought I was a student. I stepped into the room. "I'm sorry. I'm Francesca Amaro from Antonia's Italian Café. I'm scheduled to meet with you."

She looked up from her desk with unmasked irritation on her face. "This is my planning period. You need to ask before you come into my classroom."

"I'm sorry," I repeated. "May I come in?"

She waved her hand at one of the desks and looked back down at the papers in front of her. I started to pull the desk closer to hers, but she stopped me. "Leave it where it is. It took me a long time to get this room set up, and I don't appreciate people messing it up."

I pushed the desk back into place and sat down.

Not wanting to risk irritating her further, I decided to wait until she was finished with whatever she was looking at. Apparently, I decided wrong.

"Well?" she said a few seconds later without looking up.

I took a deep breath and tried to remind myself that teaching is a stressful job. This woman dealt with hormonal teenagers all day, and it was probably enough to make anyone a little testy. All I needed to do was stay calm and be reasonable, and she'd probably warm up to me in a few minutes. And it wasn't as if she was the first less-than-friendly person I'd ever dealt with. In my former life as a public relations representative, I'd dealt with more than a few celebrities who acted as though they were doing me a favor by letting my firm represent them. Most of them had at least made an attempt at being civil, though.

"As I said, I'm Francesca Amaro from Antonia's Italian Café here in town. I'm here to talk to you about setting up a refreshment stand during the play next weekend."

"Right," she said, tapping her pencil eraser on her papers and finally actually looking at me. "All the proceeds go to the drama club, and we're not paying for anything. You're donating it all."

I stared at her. They were the terms I had been

planning to offer, but my plan had been to come across as exceptionally generous by declining to take any kind of payment. I had almost collected myself enough to respond when she added her next requirement.

"And you'll need to staff it."

My mouth fell open slightly. Her presumptuousness was astounding.

"If that's a problem, we'll find someone else." Her pencil bouncing had stopped, and she stared at me as if she was daring me—whether it was to accept or decline, I didn't know.

I wanted to say no. I really did. But Antonia's had been a part of Cape Bay for going on seventy years. We'd sponsored school activities, raised money for charities, and donated our food for more events than I could count. As much as I wanted to walk out of that classroom just to spite her, it would be entirely counter to the ideals my grandparents had established from the time they first opened the café. So I smiled. "That's exactly what I was going to suggest. I'm so glad we're on the same page!"

"The play opens Friday night. I'll expect you to be set up and ready to sell an hour before show-time." She looked back down at her papers.

"That sounds great!" I said, still trying to sound cheerful. "Is there anything in particular you'd like us to serve? I brought some samples of our baked goods for you to try if you'd like." I reached into my oversized bag for the plastic container I'd loaded up with tasty pastries.

"I really don't care. As long as it sells. We need the money. I don't know what the old drama club sponsors were spending their money on, but everything we have is crap and needs to be replaced."

"Okay then."

"Is there something else, or can you go now? I have things to do that I can't get done with you sitting there."

"No, I think that's more than enough." I stood up and slid my bag over my shoulder. I waited a moment for her to say something, but when she didn't, I decided I didn't want to encourage her to since nothing she'd said yet could be described as anything more than barely civil. Still, I couldn't bring myself to be equally as rude. "I'll see you next week, then. If you decide there is anything in particular you'd like us to serve, please let me know. We'll be happy to do whatever we can."

She still said nothing.

Deciding that meant I was dismissed, I happily left the room. If I never saw that woman again after the play, I couldn't say I'd be sorry.

Chapter 2

I BROKE off a piece of gingerbread and popped it in my mouth. "Hot! Hot! Hot!" I breathed as I bounced it around, trying to keep it from burning my tongue.

Samantha Eriksen, my usually supportive right-hand woman at Antonia's Italian Café, laughed as she watched me fan my open mouth with both hands. "You never learn, do you, Fran?"

I shook my head. It wasn't the first time we'd had this conversation. It happened with pretty much every batch of cookies I made. I'd pull the tray out of the oven, smell the enticing aroma of the cookies, and not be able to help myself. The first time, Sammy had been concerned and sympathetic. Since then, she'd just laughed.

She walked over and peered at the cookie sheets with their neat lines of gingerbread men. "You went for his head first?"

"It's the most humane thing to do." The gingerbread head had finally cooled down enough that I could actually let it touch my tongue. I couldn't help but smile at the warm, spicy deliciousness of it. It was perfect.

Sammy shook her head. "It's barbaric." She was a leg person.

"You think it's better to make him watch as you eat him limb by limb?"

She shrugged. We'd had this conversation several times.

Sammy wrinkled her nose. "Well, no, but—it just seems cruel."

I laughed. "You're welcome to eat yours however you want. I like to start with the head." I snapped the head off another one and put it in my mouth. I was only smug for a second as I realized that the cookies still weren't cool enough to keep from burning me.

"That's what you get." Sammy smiled. She broke the leg off one of my victims and carefully blew on it for a few seconds before taking a bite. Her patience paid off, and she chewed and swallowed it immediately.

I, on the other hand, was still fanning at my piece, perched delicately between my teeth.

"Delicious as always," she commended me.

"Good." I managed to swallow the piece down without scalding myself and reached toward another head.

"Stop that!" Sammy swatted at my hand. "We can't sell headless ones!"

"Are you sure? What if we decorated them—"

"No!"

"What about at Halloween?"

"No—" She said it almost before the words made it out of my mouth, then cut herself off. "Okay, maybe at Halloween."

I made a mental note to make headless ginger-bread men for Halloween. Well, regular ginger-bread men that I would then have the pleasure of breaking the heads off. Maybe I could even manage to pull off some headless horsemen. We were in New England, after all.

"Do you want me to mix up the icing, or do you want to do it?" Sammy asked, interrupting my mental planning for a holiday that I really didn't need to think about for another nine months.

I glanced around the café. We were in the middle of the late-afternoon lull—after school got out but before people started stopping by on their way home from work. One of the high school students who worked for me part-time would normally have been there, but one of them was out of town visiting family before the holiday, and the other was at play practice and wouldn't be in for another hour or so. Still, Sammy and I didn't have much to do.

"How about I mix the icing and you do the coloring?" I suggested. "That way you can make sure you get the colors you want."

"Sounds good!" she said.

While I handled most of the baking for the café, only bringing in a few things from other local bakers who had specialties I couldn't improve upon, I left the cookie decorating to Sammy. I occasionally gave her suggestions like "let's do some ugly Christmas sweater gingerbread men" or "I think this one could use some more hair," but beyond that, I gave her free rein. She came up with far better designs than I ever could. The things she could do with some icing and a piping bag were remarkable.

Sammy and I made the icing as the cookies cooled, and then I left her to the decorating while I started mixing up a batch of sugar cookies.

We made and sold cookies all year round, but there was always something special to me about the cookies at Christmastime. I didn't know if it was the fond memories of spending hours baking them with my mother and grandmother or just the ritual of it, but I loved it—especially the whole process of making rolled cookies like gingerbread or sugar cookies. Making them wasn't as easy as scooping them and slapping them on a cookie sheet. Rolled cookies took time and technique. You couldn't rush them. After you mixed the dough, you had to let it chill, and then you had to roll the dough out evenly. Then there was the challenge of cutting as many shapes as possible out of the dough. And then, after they were baked and cooled, there was the decorating. The whole process was soothing, and I loved it.

"Do you think this one has too much icing?" Sammy asked, holding up a gingerbread man wearing an intricately patterned pair of Christmas-themed pajamas.

"There's no such thing as too much icing," a familiar voice behind me said.

I turned around and smiled at my boyfriend, Matt Cardosi. "What are you doing here?"

He brushed a kiss across my lips before answering. "My last meeting ended early, so I figured I'd head out before rush hour. The office is empty on Friday afternoons this close to Christmas, anyway."

"I'd hug you, but I'm a mess." I glanced from

his clean white dress shirt to my apron. It was a good thing I had it on. In addition to a liberal coating of flour, there were also a few smears of gingerbread dough. Fortunately, the apron was black, so it mostly hid the speckles of food coloring I knew also covered it.

"I see that. You'll just have to owe me." He smiled mischievously. "I do charge interest, though."

I giggled despite myself.

Matt looked over at Sammy, who had gone back to her cookie decorating. "If you're worried about that one having too much icing, I can take it off your hands for you. No charge."

"Uh-uh. No," I said as he reached over toward it. "That one's too pretty. It's going out front so our actual paying customers can see how talented Sammy is."

"Well, do you have an ugly one?" he asked, scoping out the tray that held Sammy's finished work. "I can taste test them for you. Make sure Franny didn't accidentally use salt instead of sugar."

"That only happened once!" I protested.

"Still, it's better to be safe than sorry." His hand inched toward one of the cookies. Sammy swatted at it with a towel.

"You can have one from that tray over there,"

she said, pointing to a different tray, which held my beheaded victims and the couple that she'd smudged. "But Fran's already sampled them."

Matt grinned at me. "Burn your tongue again?"

"No!"

"She's getting better," he said to Sammy.

She nodded as she glanced over at me, her lips twitching up in a smile.

"I'm ignoring you two," I said and dumped the sugar cookie dough out of the mixer bowl and onto a piece of plastic wrap for storage in the refrigerator.

"Do you want me to taste that for you?" Matt reached over with a spoon he'd grabbed from somewhere and tried to scoop off a bite of my dough.

"Matty!" I made motions as if I were trying to stop him but let him get a bite of it.

He nodded approvingly. "Tastes like sugar cookies."

I wrapped up the dough and took it to the refrigerator. I was putting the bowl and paddle from the mixer in the sink to be washed when Becky, one of my high school student part-timers, came in.

"How was play practice?" Sammy asked.

Becky shrugged as she dropped her backpack and coat off in the storage room. Sammy and I exchanged a look.

"Still having trouble with Ms. Underwood?" Sammy asked.

Becky nodded.

"At least it's almost over, right? Just another week?"

"Yeah."

Sammy and I looked at each other again. Becky was usually much more bubbly and chatty than that. She'd been a little more down than usual since play practice started, but nothing like this.

"Is everything okay?" I asked. "Did something happen at practice today?"

She shrugged and sniffed. For a second, I thought she was going to cry, but then it passed. "Ms. Underwood was yelling at us a lot today. It's really annoying. The play was always really fun when Mrs. Crowsdale and Ms. Blarney were in charge of it, but Ms. Underwood's so mean. It's like, why is she even a teacher if she thinks teenagers are so annoying, you know? Like, she volunteered to do this. It's part of her *job*. It's what the drama teacher *does*."

"Can you talk to Mrs. Crowsdale about it?" Sammy asked. Mrs. Crowsdale was the assistant director in the play and one of the most popular teachers at Cape Bay High School.

"We've tried! And she's tried to talk to Ms.

Underwood, but it doesn't make a difference. She's brand new, and she thinks she knows everything, and she doesn't listen to anybody! She tells us we're stupid and calls us entitled little brats like there's something wrong with us because we don't like being yelled at. She's just mean!" Now Becky really looked as if she was going to cry. Not that I could blame her. Based on my short experience with her, Ms. Underwood was awful.

"Aw, Becky." Sammy put down her piping bag and gave Becky a hug. "I know it's hard, but you can make it through it. The play's next week. Then it'll be over. It's just a few more days."

At least, that was what we all thought.

Chapter 3

I WOKE up late the next morning after a fun date night with Matt. We went to dinner after I closed the café for the night then caught a late showing of the newest blockbuster movie full of car chases and exploding buildings and bad guys dying in unlikely ways. It wasn't really my kind of movie, but Matt really wanted to see it, so I agreed after extracting a promise from him that he wouldn't complain about going to the next based-on-the-bestselling-novel chick flick I wanted to see.

That morning, I lolled around the house for a while with my beloved Berger Picard dog, Latte, named for his fur, which was exactly the color of a perfectly poured latte. It was one of my favorite drinks to make, in part because of the skill it took to

make a really good one. It wasn't particularly difficult to make a passable one, but I took pride in
making more than passable ones—pulling the shots
of espresso just right so that they had a beautiful,
perfect crema on top, steaming the milk to perfec-
tion, and then pouring the milk in so that it made a
beautiful design on top. I'd heard people say latte
art gets in the way of a good latte, but as far as I
was concerned, that was just an excuse. You could
have a latte that was heavenly to drink and lovely to
look at at the same time. In fact, it had been one of
my grandfather's mottos back when he and my
grandmother first opened Antonia's Italian Café
after they emigrated from Italy—"make your food
delicious, and make it beautiful." They were words
I still tried to live by, even if I had to rely on Sammy
to help me do it.

After taking Latte on a lengthy stroll around
town, I showered and headed in to the café.

Antonia's wasn't far from my house—which was
actually the reason my grandparents had bought
the house sixty-some years ago—but then, nothing
in the tiny beach town of Cape Bay was really that
far from anything else. I rarely drove anywhere
except to the grocery store, and even then, it was
only because it was easier to load my bags in the
trunk than it was to carry them.

I took the shortcut I'd taken since I was a child —out the back door, through the neighbors' yards, and out onto the street a block or so from the back door of the café. Even though we were already in the second half of December, we'd only had one snowfall that amounted to anything more than a dusting, and that was long since gone. The ground was frozen solid but completely bare, so I didn't have to deal with slogging through the snow and changing into and out of snow boots. It was pretty frigid, though—just above freezing—so I bundled up in my warmest coat, wrapped a scarf around my neck, and pulled a knit hat low on my forehead. It was the one time of year I really appreciated my thick mop of black hair—it served as a kind of bonus scarf, insulating me from the wind that was determined to cut through my regular one.

I walked in through the back door of the café, hung my coat, and divested myself of all the other trappings of winter in Massachusetts. Through the door to the café, I could see Sammy leaning across the counter, talking to her maybe-boyfriend, Officer Ryan Leary of the Cape Bay Police Department, who, I noticed, was eating his uniform-clad gingerbread man legs-first. I'd have to ask Sammy if she'd decorated a whole series of police officer gingerbread men, or if she only made one for Ryan.

Despite the fact that anyone with eyes could see that the two of them were head over heels for each other, they refused to admit that they were seeing each other. Sammy was still coming off a fairly recent breakup with her longtime loser boyfriend, but I didn't know what Ryan's aversion to publicly saying they were official was.

"Hey, guys!" I called to them through the open door.

Ryan nodded in my direction, tipping his legless gingerbread man at me. I wondered if he saw the humor in the fact that the cookie he was eating was wearing the same outfit he was.

Sammy smiled in a way that made it look almost painful.

"How's it going?" I asked. I slipped my apron over my head and walked over to where they were standing as I tied the strings behind my back.

"Got another body," Ryan said.

"Ryan!" Sammy gave him a disapproving look.

"What?" Ryan and I asked at the same time, though our tones were dramatically different—mine was shock. Ryan's was more as if he genuinely didn't know why Sammy reacted that way.

"You shouldn't act so casual about it!" Sammy said, choosing to answer Ryan first.

"Sorry," he mumbled and bit off a ginger-arm.

He had a habit of being a little too blunt talking about crimes. He forgot that not everyone was in law enforcement and dealt with it every day.

I looked between them, waiting for one of them to fill me in, but Ryan was munching, and Sammy seemed to have forgotten I was there. "So what's going on?" I asked.

Ryan glanced at Sammy.

"Go ahead," she said.

He swallowed his bite of gingerbread. "There's been another murder," he said, looking again at Sammy for her approval.

"Better," she said.

"Who?" I asked.

"Veronica Underwood. She was a teacher at the high school."

"Veronica Underwood?" I repeated. "I just saw her yesterday!"

"She was just found last night." He eyed me up and down. "I don't need to question you, do I?"

"What? No!" I replied defensively.

"Is there something you want tell me? Like where you saw her? And when?"

I couldn't imagine that he really wanted to question me, but there was always an off chance he wasn't at the café to see Sammy. Or for the free coffee, which was the other big draw for him. "At the school," I said. "I met her to talk about the bake sale we're doing during the play to support the drama club."

Ryan broke into a grin. "Relax, Fran. I'm just messing with you."

"About Ms. Underwood being dead or just about needing to question me?"

"Unfortunately, just about needing to question you. Veronica Underwood really is dead."

"Murdered."

"Yup."

"Do you have any suspects yet?"

"I know this is going to disappoint you," Ryan said, "but we do."

"Trust me, I am not disappointed," I said. There had been a handful of murders in Cape Bay over the past few months, and I'd somehow managed to get myself involved in the investigation of each of them, which was why Ryan suggested I'd be disappointed that they already had a suspect. But I'd had enough of murder investigations. I'd had enough of murders in Cape Bay in general, but since I wasn't doing any of the actual murdering, there wasn't much I could do about that. The investigations, on the other hand, had seemed to find me. If anything, I was relieved that the police had a suspect and there was no use in me getting involved, let alone any need for me to.

Before we could discuss it any further, the police radio on Ryan's shoulder crackled to life and said something completely incomprehensible. Ryan somehow understood and muttered something back into it, starting with the only thing I understood from the whole exchange: "Ten-four."

He looked at Sammy and grimaced. "Looks like I gotta go."

"You want a refill of your coffee?"

"Yes, please."

Sammy topped off his coffee cup then grabbed a blond, blue-eyed gingerbread girl, dropped it into a bag, and handed it to him with a coy smile.

Ryan took it, smiling back at her. "Thanks, Sam. See you later." I was pretty sure I saw him wink at her before he turned to me and waved. "See ya, Fran."

"See ya, Ryan."

Sammy and I watched as he left the café and turned out onto the street.

"So, Veronica Underwood," I said after he disappeared from our view.

"Yup," Sammy replied.

"Did he tell you anything about who they think did it?"

"No. He just told me she was dead right before you got here."

"Do you know how it happened?"

She shook her head.

I sighed. As unpleasant as she was, I didn't like that a woman was dead, and I really didn't like that there had been yet another murder in our small, otherwise nearly crime-free town. But even so, there was one good thing about it.

"I hate to say it, but on the bright side—" I stopped myself, still not sure I could actually bring myself to say it out loud.

Sammy finished my sentence for me. "At least Becky and the other kids don't have to deal with her anymore."

Chapter 4

IT WAS, of course, the talk of the café the rest of the day. If people weren't talking about it when they came in, they talked about it over their coffee. News travels fast in a small town, and it was no surprise that everyone knew about it and everyone had an opinion. Especially the high school students and their parents. You could almost spot them—while everyone else looked upset, or at least morbidly curious, the people who actually knew Veronica Underwood had a look that was probably best described as relief. At least everyone had the decency not to look *happy* about it.

Somehow, I managed to avoid anyone asking if I was going to do my own investigation of her murder. It continually surprised me that people outside my small circle knew about my roles in solving the previous murders, but I guess it was that small-town thing again—everyone knew everyone's business, and most of them weren't shy about asking. I didn't know whether Veronica Underwood was really so strongly disliked that nobody cared about seeing her murderer punished, or if no one had thought that far because the news about her death was still so fresh. Or maybe it was the Christmas spirit. All I knew was that no one was asking me if I was going to solve the case, and I couldn't have been happier about that. Well, maybe if no one was dead in the first place, but there was nothing I could do about that.

Naturally, it couldn't last.

It was late afternoon when Rhonda Davis came strolling in. She was about ten years older than me and had two teenage boys who, I realized, would at least know of Veronica Underwood if they didn't actually know her. Rhonda also worked for me part-time, mostly to support her shopping habit. She practically considered the Neiman Marcus up in Boston to be her second home, and that was where she'd been most of the day. Usually, she restricted her shopping trips—and her working for me—to times when her boys were in school, but with Christmas two short weeks away, she'd been expanding them to every available opportunity. She was on her way home from her latest one when she came into the café.

"Hey, girls!" she called out to Sammy and me as she breezed through the door. She was bundled in a massive parka to keep the nearly frigid December air off her.

"Hey, Rhonda!" I called back. "How was your shopping trip?" Sammy was getting ready to leave, and she and I were tucked behind the counter, discussing how many cookies I would need to make to be ready for the next day.

Rhonda sighed dreamily. "I think I could live at Neiman's if they'd let me."

Sammy and I laughed.

"That doesn't surprise me at all," I said.

"What're you girls talking about?" Rhonda asked, leaning against the counter. "How Fran's going to solve Veronica Underwood's murder?"

I groaned, and Sammy laughed.

Rhonda laughed too. "Heard that a few too many times today?"

"First time, actually," I replied.

"Wow, really? Do people think you're losing your touch or something?"

"Maybe they just want to give me a break and let me act like a normal citizen for once."

"Actually, Ryan said that the police already have a suspect. That's probably why people aren't asking Fran about it," Sammy said.

Rhonda looked pointedly at Sammy and raised an eyebrow. "Not everyone has the intimate access to the police that you do, Sammy."

Sammy's face turned bright red. "Oh, well, I, uh, I just—"

"Rhonda was just teasing you," I said, giving Rhonda a look and patting Sammy on the back. For some reason, Sammy could never tell when Rhonda was joking.

"So who do they think did it?" Rhonda asked.

"We don't know," I said then looked at Sammy. "Unless you've heard?"

She shook her head, her blush subsiding.

"Yeah, we don't know."

Rhonda's phone rang. She looked at it and sighed then tapped the screen and held it to her head. "Hello, Dan."

It was her husband. She "yeah," "yup," and "uh-huh'ed" her way through the conversation before ending with "I'm just going to grab a cup of coffee at the café, and then I'll be home." She ended the call and dropped her phone back in her handbag. "Guess it's time for Mom to get back to work." She sighed.

"A latte?" I asked, grabbing a to-go cup.

"Yup."

I put the to-go cup in its place and started pulling the espresso shot before steaming the milk. When everything was ready, I poured the milk into the espresso, flicking my wrist just so to coax out the image I wanted. I dipped a toothpick into the spare steamed milk and scooped out some of the micro-foam. I dabbed it into Rhonda's latte, adding in the finishing accents. When it was done, I rotated it around to face Rhonda, turning it carefully to keep from mixing the crisp white of the milk into the warm brown of the crema.

"That's the best latte Christmas tree I've ever seen," she said. "I almost don't want to mess it up by drinking it."

"It tastes even better than it looks."

She took a sip, skewing the Christmas tree slightly. She nodded as she put it down. "That's exactly what I needed." She glanced at the cookie case. "And actually, I think I need one of those snowflake cookies too."

I slid open the display case and pulled out one of the snowflake-shaped sugar cookies that Sammy had iced in an intricate geometric pattern then dusted with white and silver edible glitter. They were outstandingly pretty. "Do you want it in a bag?"

"Oh, no. I need to eat it before I get home, or I might as well buy a dozen. You'd think we never feed those boys the way they attack anything I bring in the house."

I handed her the cookie, and she immediately took a bite. She groaned as she chewed on it. "Now, that is a good cookie."

"Anything else?"

"Oh, I should probably get an Americano for Dan."

I made her an Americano then put both drinks in a drink carrier for her.

"Oh, what the heck. I guess you may as well give me a dozen cookies. The boys will feel left out if I bring something for their dad and not for them."

"Christmas presents don't count?" I asked.

She laughed. "Only on Christmas day."

I selected a variety of the cookies—gingerbread men and Christmas trees, sugar cookie snowflakes and candy canes, plus a few others, all gorgeously decorated—and handed it to her.

"All right." She paid and picked everything up. "I'd better go before one of the boys texts to find out where I am."

"They won't ask Dan?"

"Oh, no, of course not. That would make way too much sense. They're probably both hidden up in their rooms, texting or playing video games. But even if they're not, neither of them actually talks anymore—they just grunt." She sighed. "You know, when your kids are babies, people joke with you that you can't wait for them to start talking and then, once they do, you can't wait for them to stop. And you know what? They're right. A kid can wear you out like you wouldn't believe asking 'why' every three seconds. But the thing they don't tell you is that, once they get to be teenagers, they turn into modern cavemen, just pointing and grunting all the time. I'd gladly trade that nonstop chatter they used to do as toddlers for this caveman phase they're in now." She shook her head then held up the bag of cookies. "If I'm lucky, these'll get me a 'Thanks, Mom.'" She sighed again. "Oh well. They'll grow out of it. I'll see you girls Monday!"

Sammy and I watched her leave.

"What were we talking about?" I asked her after Rhonda was gone.

"Have you thought about getting involved in the investigation?" she asked.

"I'm pretty sure that's not what we were talking about."

"I know, but I started thinking about it while you and Rhonda were talking."

"You said it yourself," I said. "The police already have a suspect. They don't need my help." A split second went by before I thought of something else. "Besides, I've had enough of amateur police work."

Sammy nodded, but I could see on her face that she was still thinking about it.

I didn't want to talk about it anymore, though, so I went back to what we really had been talking about before Rhonda came in. "So we decided on four dozen gingerbread and three dozen sugar cookies for tomorrow, right? Any particular shapes you want?"

"People seem to like the snowflakes. And the snowmen. And the Christmas trees."

"And the ornaments and the gingerbread men and the houses and—"

Sammy laughed. "Yeah, I guess they're all pretty popular."

"I'll just make a bunch of different ones. Whatever fits best on the cookie sheet."

"Sounds good." She looked over at the big wrought iron clock on the exposed brick wall across from us. "Oh, I need to go."

She hurried to the back for her coat and bag, then we said goodbye and she left.

A few hours later, just before closing, Matt and I were alone in the café. I was baking cookies, and Matt was keeping me company. It was partly him just being a sweet boyfriend—something that came naturally to him—and partly that I was still a little anxious about walking home by myself at night after I'd been followed during the last police investigation I'd gotten myself involved in back before Thanksgiving. It worked out for both of us—I didn't have to walk alone, and Matt got all the cookies and other goodies he could eat.

I was just about to tell Matt to go ahead and lock the door when it swung open. In with a cold gust of wind came Mrs. D'Angelo.

"Francesca, darling! Have you heard the news?" She was standing in front of me, gripping my arms with her long clawlike red fingernails, almost before I realized she'd come in. For an older woman, she was fast. "Did Matteo tell you? Matteo, have you heard?" I didn't think I'd ever heard her call anyone anything but their full names. I was Francesca, Matt was Matteo, and Sammy was Samantha. Always.

"I heard about the murder, yes, Mrs. D'Angelo," I managed to get in. With Mrs. D'Angelo, it wasn't always easy.

"No, not the *murder*, Francesca! Of course you've heard about that! No, the *news*! They've made an arrest!"

"Already?"

"That Michael Stanton is so good at his job! I wasn't sure about him—didn't know if he'd ever amount to anything back when you all were growing up, but he's really made something of himself. Really done well. And that Sandra. He did well to marry her. His parents should be proud of him for landing a lovely girl like her. Their children are just precious too. What are their names again? Oh, I don't know. I can never remember! So many little ones running around these days, it's hard for me to remember all their names. But that's neither here nor there. I do need to be getting along. I've been dealing with preparations for the Ladies' Auxiliary's Christmas luncheon all day, and I'm positively exhausted! Good night, Francesca! Good night, Matteo!" She bustled back toward the door, leaving me with what I was sure were deep-red crescents in my arms where she had held them. I realized she hadn't said whom the police actually arrested.

"Mrs. D'Angelo!" I called.

"Yes, Francesca?" She whirled back around at the door. For a second, I thought she was going to come back over and re-embed her nails in my upper arms, but mercifully, she stayed where she was.

"You said the police made an arrest. Who was it?"

"Oh!" she said. "You'll never believe it! Ann Crowsdale, dear!" And before I could say anything else, she was gone, leaving nothing but her news and a cloud of her heavy floral perfume in her wake.

Chapter 5

THE MOOD in the café the next day was unusually subdued. The excited, gossipy hum from the day before had been completely replaced by a hushed murmur. People were stunned that Ann Crowsdale had been arrested. I overheard more than one person say that they couldn't believe it, that she wouldn't do such a thing, that she was incapable of it. I even heard someone say once or twice that they thought the police had it wrong.

I didn't know Ann Crowsdale personally, but by all accounts, she was a lovely woman. Well, lovely, that was, except for the thing about possibly being a murderer. I did know Mike Stanton, though, the Cape Bay Police Department's lead detective. He was the lucky one who got to investigate all the most serious crimes—the murders, the assaults, the art thefts. Despite butting heads with him a few times over me getting involved with his cases, or maybe because of that, I knew he was a good detective and not prone to jumping to conclusions. If Mike had arrested Ann Crowsdale, it was because he had good evidence that she did it.

That didn't make much difference to all the people who knew and loved her and didn't believe —or want to believe—that she was a murderer, my staff included. Sammy's eyes were rimmed in red, and she was far from her normal bubbly self. She was helping the customers, but her smile was gone. Becky seemed aimless and distracted. She was doing her job but with none of her usual spark and verve. The two of them barely acknowledged me when I came in, with Sammy just giving me a wan smile and Becky a half-hearted wave. Sammy had decorated the cookies I'd made the night before, and they were well done, but they had none of the details she usually included—no sugar crystal sprin-kles, no edible glitter, no fine piping that astounded me with its delicacy. Clearly, they were taking Ann Crowsdale's arrest hard.

When I got the chance, shortly after I noticed a customer had to ask her twice for napkins that she normally would have given them with their order, I pulled Sammy into the back room to talk to her. I wasn't upset with her—just concerned about how distracted she seemed.

"Are you okay?" I asked.

Sammy drew in a long, deep breath and then let it out quickly. She bit her lip and stared into space somewhere over my shoulder. Finally, she looked at me. "Yeah, I'm just—I just—" She sighed. "I'm just a little upset about Mrs. Crowsdale. I'm sorry. I shouldn't be letting it affect my work like this. I'll do better."

"Sammy, I'm not mad at you. I genuinely want to know if you're okay."

She nodded unenthusiastically. "Yeah, I am. I mean, I guess."

"Do you want to talk about it?"

She shrugged.

I weighed my options. On the one hand, I wanted her to know that I was there for her if she wanted to talk. I knew from experience that Sammy, always so sweet and compassionate and concerned for other people, sometimes needed a little push to open up because she didn't want to burden other people with her problems. On the other hand, I hadn't actually known her well for all that long, and I didn't want to make her feel uncomfortable.

"Sammy, I'm your friend," I said, deciding that

was encouraging enough if she needed a little push and neutral enough if she really didn't want to share.

She stopped studying our shoes and looked up at me. "Fran, it's just that—" She took a deep, shaky breath. "Mrs. Crowsdale was my favorite teacher. By far. She never made me feel bad that I wasn't a very good writer or I didn't like to read Shakespeare. She helped me find books I do like to read. She encouraged me to try out for the school plays. She listened whenever I had some teenage problem that I thought was impossible for adults to understand and I could never solve. She was like a mentor. And it wasn't just me. She did—still does—more to help her students than any other teacher I've ever seen. And she organizes the blood drives and the food drives and the toy drives for kids at Christmas." Her voice broke, and she choked back a sob. "This is the most important week for the toy drive. Who's going to coordinate everything if she's in jail? What if she doesn't get out in time for Christmas? Her husband—her kids—" Sammy covered her face and started crying.

I rubbed her arm and then pulled her into a hug until she calmed down a little.

"I'm sorry," she said, leaning against the edge of the desk.

"Don't be. It sounds like she's a really lovely person, and this has to be a shock."

Sammy nodded. "I just don't see how she could have done it. It's not like her. Not to be angry or violent or anything like that."

"Have you found out anything about how Veronica Underwood was killed?"

Sammy sniffled. "She was hit in the temple with a tire iron. In the school parking lot. But I just can't believe that Mrs. Crowsdale would do something like that. I won't believe it."

"Sammy, the police wouldn't have arrested her if they didn't have good evidence that she did it."

"I don't care what the police have! Mrs. Crowsdale wouldn't have done something like that. She couldn't have. It's just not who she is!"

I wanted to tell her that people do surprising things sometimes, things you'd never believe or expect, and for reasons that don't necessarily make sense to other people. I wanted to say that you never really know what people are capable of until they show you. But I realized it wasn't the place or the time. Whether Mrs. Crowsdale had done it or not, Sammy was upset, and my job as her friend was to support her.

"Have you talked to Ryan about it?"

"He won't talk about it. He says it's because it's

an active case, but I think he just doesn't want to. I tried to tell him that Mrs. Crowsdale wouldn't do something like that, but——" She shrugged. "He says it was Mike's call." She sniffled again. "I should get back to work."

I looked at Sammy's teary eyes and mascara-streaked face. "Do you want to go ahead and take a break for a few minutes? Maybe splash some cold water on your face?"

"Do I look that bad?" she asked.

"No, just——" I drew imaginary tear streaks down my cheeks with my fingers.

Sammy grimaced. "I guess maybe I should take a couple of minutes."

"I'll go help Becky. But if you want to talk more later, or if you need an extra break or two, just let me know, okay?"

"Thanks, Fran. You're a good friend."

I walked out into the café and quickly stepped aside so Becky could walk by me with a tray of drinks.

"Whoa, whoa, whoa! What's that?" I asked, looking down at what looked like a very small cup of plain coffee.

"It's an espresso?" Becky said, or asked if you went by her inflection.

"But it has no crema. How long has that been sitting? You can't serve an espresso with no crema."

I didn't think the tone in my voice was anything other than matter-of-fact, but Becky looked up at me, her eyes wide, and started sobbing. She pushed the tray into me and ran into the back room, banging the door closed behind her.

I stood there in shock for a few seconds before I realized that everyone in the café—and I do mean everyone—was staring at me. I tried to smile, even as I felt a flush creeping up my cheeks. "Sorry about that!" I announced to the café. "She's just having a rough day. Now whose drinks do I have here? It looks like a latte, a cappuccino, an espresso—" A table at the far end of the café raised their hands. Of course. Because the one time all of my customers think I'm an ogre who makes my employees cry, I have to walk past every single one of them to deliver what I was afraid were going to be cold drinks. I took a deep breath and made my way down to the table.

"Okay, I have a cappuccino—"

A man raised his hand, and I passed it to him.

"A latte?" I noticed Becky hadn't even poured a rosetta into the latte's crema. It wasn't necessarily something I required my staff to do, but I felt that we were known for details like that, so I was a little bit disappointed that Becky had overlooked it, especially since I knew she'd been practicing her pour. I passed the latte to the woman who raised her hand.

I looked at the remaining man at the table. "And I'm so sorry, but this espresso has been sitting longer than I'd like it to, so I'm going to get you a fresh one." I looked at his two companions. "And if either of you aren't satisfied with your drinks, let me know, and I'll make you fresh ones also. My name is Fran, and I'm the owner. Please feel free to ask me if you need anything."

I went back behind the counter to make the man a fresh espresso then delivered it to the table along with a pile of cookies for their trouble. I checked in at several tables to make sure everyone was okay then went to the door into the back room. I was actually a little surprised that it was unlocked.

I tapped on the door and poked my head in. Becky was sitting at the table, her head down, her shoulders shaking with sobs. Sammy sat next to her, rubbing her back.

"Can I come in?" I asked. It felt a little strange asking if I could enter my own office, but it was a strange day.

Sammy looked up at me and nodded.

I pulled up a chair and sat down next to Becky. "Are you okay?"

She looked up at me. Her eyes were puffy and red, and she had mascara rivers down her cheeks. If Sammy hadn't already cleaned herself up, they would have been twins. She sniffled and nodded. "Yeah, I'm just—I'm just really upset about Mrs. Crowsdale," she said through her sobs. "And now you're mad at me."

"I'm not mad at you."

"But I screwed up the drinks! I let that espresso sit too long, and I forgot to put the art in the latte!" She dropped her head and sobbed on my shoulder.

I patted her back awkwardly. I was getting used to managing teenage girls and had dealt with a few tears a couple of times before, but this level of crying was new to me. Well, not the crying itself— I'd shed more than a few hysterical tears when my mother passed away a few months earlier—but having my employee cry like that on my shoulder was completely new. It had been fifteen years since I was a teenage girl, and I couldn't remember what teenage me would have wanted an adult to do in that kind of situation.

I caught Sammy's eye. She smiled encouragingly and nodded. Apparently sympathetic patting at the very least wasn't the *wrong* thing to do.

Gradually, Becky's sobs subsided. She sat up and wiped at her face with the heels of her hands, smearing her mascara into something that resembled abstract art.

"I'm sorry," she said. "It's just the *worst* day. I didn't even want to come in today, but my dad said I had to."

I wanted to tell her that she never *had* to come in, that if she wasn't feeling up to it, she could always call out, but I was afraid that would backfire and lead to her calling out a little too often. My previous job had been more about managing egos and the press than employees, so I was still trying to feel out the line between being supportive and being completely lax. I decided to try for neutrality. "Well, I appreciate you coming in and giving it your best."

I glanced at Sammy. She'd worked with Becky longer than I had—it had only been a few months since I'd come back to Cape Bay to run the café—so I figured she knew better than I did how to handle the situation. She smiled. I was still doing okay.

"Do you think you're up to finishing your shift?" I asked Becky. "Or do you need to go home?"

She thought for a minute. I suspected she was debating what her dad would say about her coming home early more than she was contemplating how effectively she could finish the day, but at her age, what my family would have thought was probably more important to me too. Of course, my family and my bosses had been the same people back then, so it was a little different.

"I think I can stay," she said finally.

I gave her what I hoped was a big, supportive smile. "Great! Why don't you take a few more minutes to calm down, splash some cold water on your face, and then you can get back to work." I couldn't remember the last time I'd suggested to two people in less than thirty minutes that they splash cold water on their faces. It seemed like such a cliché thing to say or do. But maybe it got to be a cliché because it worked.

"Okay," Becky said and wiped under her eyes, smearing her remaining mascara into what actually looked almost like an intentional style.

"Okay!" I took a deep breath, slapped my hands on my legs, and got up to go back out into the café. I had a feeling it was going to be a very long few hours before the end of the day.

Chapter 6

MATT CAME to keep me company again that night while I baked cookies after closing time. As I mixed and rolled and cut the cookies, I filled him in on how weird the day had been with Sammy and Becky both breaking into tears and customers all so shocked about Ann Crowsdale's arrest.

"So this Mrs. Crowsdale is pretty popular, huh?" he asked as he bit off a gingerbread man's head, just as I did. I knew I loved that man.

"Massively. Sammy told me about all the charity things she does and how much all the students love her."

"She wasn't there when we were there, was she?" Matt and I had attended and graduated from

Cape Bay High School what seemed like an eternity ago now.

"She came our senior year."

He looked at me curiously.

I shrugged and smiled. "Last night, after you fell asleep in the middle of the movie you insisted we watch, I dug out my old yearbooks. Mrs. Bayless and Mrs. Crawford—do you remember the school secretaries?"

He shrugged and bit off a ginger-leg.

"Anyway, they said that they thought she was there when we were, so I was curious. It turns out she started when we were seniors, but she only taught freshman English. And it was before she got married, so she was Miss Chambliss back then."

"How'd you know it was her then?"

"Well, the first names were the same, so that was one clue, but I also, uh—" I paused and focused on cutting out cookies, hoping he would forget I had been talking.

"You also, uh, what?" His warm brown eyes twinkled at me. The corner of his mouth quirked up in half a smile. He knew I had been on the verge of confessing something embarrassing.

"Nothing. I could just tell they were the same person."

"You could just tell, huh?" He crammed the rest of the cookie in his mouth and came around the counter to where I was standing. He slipped his arms around my waist and brushed a kiss against my neck.

"Mm-hmm," I murmured, forgetting about the cookies.

"You could just tell?" He kissed my neck again.

"Uh-huh."

Planting delicate kisses all down my neck, he slid his hands across my belly to my hips. I wasn't even holding the cookie cutter anymore. My fingers just held onto the cool granite counter. His hands slid up to my waist… and he started tickling me. "You could just tell, huh? You could just tell?"

I screamed and jumped away from him, giggling. "Yes! I could just tell!"

"Are you sure?" He wiggled his fingers at me.

"Yes!"

I tried to back away from him and ran straight into the wall.

"Are you sure?" he repeated. He was close enough that he could tickle me again if he wanted to.

"Yes," I said again but with a little less certainty in my voice.

He wiggled his fingers then went for my sides.

I squealed again, but I couldn't jump away this

time. "Okay, okay! I'll tell!" I was laughing so hard I could barely catch my breath.

He held his hands up but didn't move away. I could tell by the light in his eyes that he'd be more than happy to resume tickling at a moment's notice.

Still, I mumbled my answer.

"What was that? I couldn't hear you." He stepped closer, so close that I could feel the warmth of his body.

"I said," I said out loud and then mumbled the rest.

He wiggled his fingers in front of his face.

I kissed him.

"Not so fast, missy." He pulled his mouth away but left his hands resting on my waist, whether for kissing or tickling, I wasn't sure.

I gave him my best puppy dog eyes.

He wiggled his fingers.

"I compared her picture in her mug shot online to the picture of her in my yearbook! Except for looking about fifteen years younger in the yearbook picture, they looked the same!"

"That's it?"

"Well, and I looked her up online, and she has her maiden name listed on her social media."

Matt smiled. The little crow's-feet at the corners of his eyes were so hot. "If all you did was look at a couple of online search results, why were you trying so hard not to tell me?"

"Well, it seemed a little—"

"Like exactly what you've done on every other murder case you've investigated?"

"I'm not investigating this case."

"Are you sure?"

"The police already have it solved."

"Mm-hmm, and you looked her up online like probably everybody else in town did."

"True," I said, although I was only barely listening to what he said. He was so warm and so close to me and his breath smelled like fresh gingerbread.

"So what's to be embarrassed about?" he asked softly in my ear.

"It just seemed like—" I sort of forgot what I was going to say next.

"A good way to get me to come kiss you?"

That sounded like a good answer. "Mm-hmm."

"You could have just asked."

He was still kissing me when someone knocked on the glass front door of the café.

"We're closed!" I called, pulling Matt's head back down to mine.

"Fran, it's me!"

Matt stepped back, and I went to let Sammy in.

"Why didn't you just use your key?" I asked her.

She looked at me skeptically. "The front of the café is a bunch of glass windows, Fran."

I blushed as I realized that anybody who had walked by could have seen Matt and me making out. Thank goodness Cape Bay was a sleepy little town that shut down early.

"Hey, Matt!" Sammy called.

"Hey, Sam!" Matt had helped himself to another cookie and was, annoyingly, looking more pleased with himself than embarrassed.

"So what's up?" I asked, hoping to move the conversation along. "You don't usually come by after we close." I thought for a second. I wasn't usually in the café long after close, so I didn't actually know. "Do you?"

"No," she said, looking at me as if it were an exceptionally strange thing to suggest. "I saw the lights on and saw you and, um, Matt in here…" She had the grace to look a little uncomfortable. "And thought maybe I could talk to you for a few minutes." She looked from me to Matt and back as though she was gauging how dismayed we were by the interruption. Not that I wouldn't have minded making out with Matt awhile longer, but I did have cookies to make, so I wasn't too bothered. Besides, I really didn't want her to think that we were routinely hooking up in the café.

"Sure," I said. "Do we need to go in the back or—"

"No, Matt's okay."

"So what's up?" I said again.

"I know we talked about it earlier, but I can't stop thinking about Mrs. Crowsdale."

"Okay," I said, picking up the cookie cutter I'd laid aside earlier.

"Hang on," she said and disappeared into the back.

I looked over at Matt. He shrugged and bit into a fresh cookie. How he ate so many without going into sugar shock, I had no idea.

Sammy reemerged with her apron on and her tray of icing supplies in her hands. "If I'm here, I may as well work," she said

"You don't have to do that," I said.

She shrugged and attached one of the tips to her piping bag. "It's less to do in the morning. Besides, I think better when I have something to occupy my hands."

"Up to you," I said as I started moving the cut cookies onto the baking sheet. "So you said you were thinking about Mrs. Crowsdale."

Sammy leaned in close to a gingerbread man as

she piped a Christmas sweater on him. "I just can't stop. I'll manage to distract myself for maybe five minutes, and then I remember that she was arrested, and I get upset all over again."

"That's understandable." I rolled out the scraps of dough left over from the batch I'd just cut out. "She's someone you look up to. It's hard to see our heroes fall."

"That's the thing, Fran." She switched piping bags and started working on the gingerbread man's pants. "No matter how hard I try, I really can't believe that she 'fell.' Not as far as murder anyway. I mean, if someone told me she'd lied about something or even shoplifted, I'd be disappointed and have trouble believing it, but murder? I just can't make myself believe she's capable of taking a life."

"Maybe it was an accident."

"She would have called 9-1-1."

"Maybe she hit Veronica on purpose but didn't mean to kill her, or even really hurt her."

"She still would have called 9-1-1."

"You don't know that, Sammy."

"No, that's the thing, Fran. I do."

"*How* do you know?" I asked. I didn't want to be argumentative, but I also didn't think she would have come to me if she wanted someone who would just blindly agree with her.

She sighed heavily. "I don't know, but I just do. I *know* she wouldn't have killed her on purpose, and I *know* that if she'd done it accidentally, she would have turned herself in."

"Are you sure she didn't turn herself in?"

She put down her piping bag and nodded. "Ryan told me," she said softly. "He said her kids were there. Mike took her outside and didn't handcuff her until they got to the car, but they still saw the police come for their mom."

"Oh wow."

Even Matt stopped munching on cookies long enough to appreciate how awful it was.

"Speaking of Ryan, have you talked to him about any of this?" I asked.

"I tried. But he said the evidence all overwhelmingly points to her."

"I'm sorry, Sammy."

"Thanks." She sighed and looked down at the cookies in front of her. "Fran, I have something to ask you."

I held my cookie cutter over the dough and rotated it back and forth, trying to figure out how I could get the most cookies out of it. "Sure, what is it?"

"Would you please investigate Veronica Underwood's murder?"

Chapter 7

I PUT down my cookie cutter and looked at Sammy.

"Sammy, you just said that all the police's evidence points to Mrs. Crowsdale," I said.

"I know," Sammy said. "But you find things the police don't. And people talk to you."

I just stared at her, not knowing what to say.

"Please, Fran?"

I really didn't want to get myself involved in another murder investigation. The last couple times I'd stuck my nose in police business, I'd found my life and my property in danger. I wasn't really interested in getting myself in either of those situations again. And I trusted Mike and Ryan and the rest of the Cape Bay Police Department. If they said all the evidence pointed to Ann Crowsdale, I believed that it did. But what if Sammy's gut feeling was right?

I looked over at Matt. He raised his eyebrows and shrugged. It looked as if I was on my own on this one. I turned back to Sammy, who stared at me imploringly.

"Sammy, I——" I started, fully intending to say no. But the look on her face was so desperate and so hopeful, I couldn't do it. "I'll think about it."

"Thank you," she said and gave me a hug.

She finished icing the group of cookies she was working on, and I got the last of my batch into and then out of the oven. We locked up the café, and then Matt and I walked Sammy to her apartment above one of the shops on Main Street.

"So," he said as we started toward our street where our houses—the houses we'd grown up in and ended up living in again in our adulthood—were two doors apart.

"So?" I asked.

"So what're you going to do?"

I sighed and leaned into him. He put his arm around me and rested his hand on my shoulder. "I really don't know," I said.

"Do you think Mike could have gotten it wrong?"

"I don't know. He's a good detective, but every

single person I've talked to or even overheard has said that there's no way Ann Crowsdale could be a murderer. They don't have the evidence Mike does, though." I gave up trying to rationalize it and shrugged. "I don't know."

"You'll figure it out," he said and kissed me on the temple. "You always do."

But by the next morning, I still hadn't. At the café, I didn't avoid Sammy, but I didn't seek her out to talk about anything other than work, either. Eventually, of course, things slowed down to the point that I couldn't avoid it any longer.

"Have you decided if you're going to investigate the murder?" she asked hopefully.

I took a deep breath, hoping that it would give me sudden clarity. It didn't. "I'm still thinking about it."

Her face fell. "Okay," she said. "I understand. But you're going to keep thinking about it?"

"Yes. I just need some more time. After everything that happened before, I just need some more time."

I could tell she was disappointed, but she took a deep breath and nodded, her long blond ponytail bobbing. "That's fine. I just—I just don't want to think about her sitting in jail any longer than she has to, you know?"

As if on cue, the bell over the door jingled, signaling a new customer.

"Oh my God," Sammy breathed then ran over to the couple who had just walked in. She hugged the woman, who started to cry.

At first, I tried to think of whether I'd ever heard of Sammy having any long-lost family members, but I looked again at the woman's face and realized with a start who she was—Ann Crowsdale.

I recognized her from the pictures I'd seen online, but only barely. Even though the mug shot had only been taken a couple of days before, she looked another fifteen years older standing in front of me than she had in the picture. Even beyond the dark circles under her eyes, she looked tired. It was in the way she held herself or, at the moment, Sammy, since they were still hugging. It was as though she was hanging on to Sammy for dear life. And she looked old, as if she'd aged two decades, the way presidents look massively older after their terms are up.

I knew from the newspaper that she'd been in jail since her arrest—the courts had been closed for the weekend, so she'd had to wait until they reopened for her arraignment. She must have gotten out on bail. She was wearing the same blue shirt that she had been in her mug shot, and I realized she and the man she was with—her husband, I guessed—had come straight to the café.

"Fran! Fran! Come over here!" Sammy called, beckoning me toward them. I noticed that she'd been crying too.

I thought I knew Sammy well enough to be sure she wouldn't put me on the spot and tell them she'd asked me to find evidence that someone else had killed Veronica Underwood, but I still had an inkling of fear that that was exactly what she was going to do. Still, I plastered my best café-owner smile on my face and walked over.

"Fran, this is Mrs. Crowsdale," Sammy said excitedly.

"Sammy, I've told you a million times! You're not my student anymore; you can call me Ann."

"It just feels so strange," Sammy said.

Ann Crowsdale smiled at her, then me, lighting up her whole face, and extended her hand. "You can call me Ann too, Fran. It's good to meet you. I was so sorry to hear about your mother. She was such a lovely person. She helped me out many times with charity events I was working on."

I was speechless for a moment as I shook her hand. This woman had just been released from jail after being arrested for either a crime she didn't commit or actually murdering someone, and the first words out of her mouth upon meeting me were to tell me she was sorry to hear about my mother's death. Finally, I managed to get my mouth to make words. "Thank you. Sammy's told me a lot about you."

"Good things, I hope."

"Very good things," I replied.

"Oh, and this is my husband, Mark," she said, gesturing toward him.

He looked tired too, but I didn't have a recent picture of him to compare to see if that was any different from usual. I suspected it was, though.

We shook hands and exchanged pleasantries, then realizing they probably hadn't come in just to meet me, I asked what I could get for them.

"Do you know what you want, hon?" Mark asked his wife.

She looked up at the menu board, which Sammy had painstakingly decorated with a winter wonderland full of snowmen, Christmas trees, reindeer grazing, and even a tiny Santa Claus flying over the top in his sleigh.

"Do you still have those delicious pumpkin spice lattes?"

"We do," I replied. I was proud of our pumpkin spice lattes. I'd eschewed the typical pumpkin spice syrup and made my own toasted spice mix, blending it with actual pumpkin to make the flavoring. It had been incredibly popular since we introduced it.

"I'd like one of those, please. A very large one of those."

"And for you?" I asked Mark.

"Espresso. A double. At least."

I wondered if the poor man had gotten any sleep at all since his wife had been arrested.

"A pumpkin spice and a double espresso. Anything else?"

I saw Ann eyeing the cookie display.

"Some cookies maybe?"

She smiled. "Maybe one or two."

I went back behind the counter to make the drinks as Sammy led the Crowsdales over to the table with the big armchairs in the back corner. Once everything was ready, I carried it all over to the table. A pumpkin spice latte decorated with a star in our very largest cup for Ann, a double espresso with an absolutely gorgeous, thick, creamy crema for Mark, and a plate piled high with cookies for the table. "I know you said one or two," I said as I put it down, "but you looked like you could use a plateful."

Ann broke into a smile as she surveyed the

mountain of cookies. She took one of the glittery snowflake sugar cookies and bit into it. She closed her eyes. "That is so good." She took a sip of her latte, and I watched as she swirled it around her mouth before swallowing. She sighed. "That is exactly what I needed."

Mark took down his double espresso in three sips that would have made my espresso-connoisseur Italian grandfather proud.

"Can I get you another?" I asked.

He hesitated for a moment. "I probably shouldn't. I haven't slept much the past few days, but I might as well."

I turned to go make his next drink but stopped when I heard him suddenly say "Oh!" When I turned around, he was reaching in his back pocket.

"Oh, no," I said. "No, no, no. None of that. It's on the house."

"But—"

"No. Please. Consider it my good deed for the day."

"Well, then let us pay for the next customer."

I looked around the café. There was no one in line and no one on the street who might conceivably be coming in any time soon. "We're a little slow right now, so I don't think you need to worry about that."

He sighed and put his wallet back into his pocket. "Well, thank you."

"Yes, thank you so much," Ann said. "I was so worried about coming out in public, about what people would think, and you have been so very, very kind. I can't thank you enough."

"Everyone knows you didn't do it, Mrs. Crows —I mean Ann," Sammy said. "We all support you."

Ann's eyes filled with tears. She clutched Sammy's hand. "I didn't, you know. I didn't—" she swallowed hard and took a breath, as if she didn't want to say the word "—kill her. I would never do something like that."

"We know," Sammy said. "The police got it wrong. It'll all be straightened out soon, I'm sure."

"I hope so," Ann said.

I went back behind the counter to get Mark his drink. Sammy sat with the Crowsdales until they left. When they were gone, she cleared their table then came up to me with a folded up napkin.

"I found this on their table," she said, handing it to me.

I unfolded the napkin and found a twenty-dollar bill inside with a note. *For the next customers.* I stared at it for a moment then looked at Sammy. "Okay, I'll do it."

Chapter 8

DESPITE AGREEING to investigate Veronica
Underwood's possibly already-solved murder, I still
wasn't sure whether I should really do it. After
meeting Ann, I understood why everyone was so
convinced she couldn't have done it. She and Mark
were both so nice, so thoughtful, that I found myself
wanting to do whatever I could to help them.

But it felt strange to do it when the police had
already closed the case. If they had looked at all
their evidence and all their information and come
up with Ann Crowsdale, how likely was I to find
something different? And if I did, would they
believe me? And how mad would Mike be about
me poking around? It already drove him nuts when
I investigated open cases. Then again, maybe he

would actually be more okay with it since the case was already closed. If it didn't hurt his ego too much.

I was glad the café had gotten pretty steadily busy after the Crowsdales left. It kept me occupied and gave me an excuse not to be out pounding the pavement yet in search of clues. Based on the way Sammy kept glancing my way every time things slowed down the slightest bit, I could tell she was eager for me to get out there. I needed to think first, though. About the case, about who to talk to, and about how on earth anything I found was going to make the slightest difference.

Becky came in after school looking tired and stressed, but at least she didn't look as if she was going to burst into tears.

"How was school?" Sammy asked her.

She shrugged. "It sucked."

"It must have been a rough day, being the first day back since Ms. Underwood…died," I said. "I heard they were going to have grief counselors in case anyone needed someone to talk to."

She laughed. "Yeah, and they were really annoyed that everyone wanted to talk about how upset they were about Mrs. Crowsdale instead of Ms. Underwood."

I stood there for a second, trying to think of the

adult thing to say. Obviously, I didn't want to encourage their "ding dong, the witch is dead" attitude, but on the other hand, I had met the woman. And I'd met Ann Crowsdale. I couldn't say I was surprised that the kids were more upset about one of them than the other. "Well, you can certainly grieve over someone being arrested," I said finally, deciding that that sounded sufficiently noncommittal.

"It's a lot sadder than Ms. Underwood getting killed."

"Becky!" Sammy and I said at the same time. We all knew it; we were all thinking it; Sammy and I just knew better than to say it out loud.

"What?" Becky asked innocently, as if she really had no idea.

Sammy and I looked at each other. She shrugged and made an "I don't know" gesture. I sighed. I was going to have to be the adult.

"Even if you didn't like her, she's still a person, and she was still murdered. That's a tragedy no matter what she was like. And whoever killed her needs to be punished, no matter who it was. Murder is wrong, period." I felt like a moralizing harpy, but I couldn't very well let it go without saying anything.

"Oh my gosh, Fran, I know! I'm not stupid. I

was just saying that I like Mrs. Crowsdale a lot more than I ever liked Ms. Underwood, not that I thought she deserved to *die*. Geez, what kind of person do you think I am?" She rolled her eyes and headed for the back room to drop off her bag.

I was glad, because I didn't have any idea what to say next.

She came back out a minute later with her apron on. "And it's not even like that's the worst thing anybody said about Ms. Underwood today either. I mean, some kids didn't even try to act like they weren't happy she's dead."

Sammy and I exchanged a glance.

"Like who?" I asked.

"OMG, Brett Wallace."

She actually said the letters O-M-G out loud, and I suddenly felt very old. I forced myself to move past it, though. "He seemed happy about Ms. Underwood dying?"

"Yeah, but he's pretty messed up in general, though."

Sammy and I exchanged another look.

"Messed up? How?"

"He's just into weird stuff. And he's, like, aggressive and stuff. Especially with girls. He likes to grab us and stuff."

"He *grabs you*?" I was now not just interested in

whether he could have killed Veronica Underwood but horrified that he was *grabbing* the girls.

"Just on the arm usually. It's more to scare us than anything. It's like he wants us to be afraid of him or something."

"Are you afraid of him?"

Becky shrugged. She didn't seem bothered or afraid in the slightest, but I knew teenage girls were masters of indifference. "I mean, I wouldn't want to be alone with him or anything."

"Because you think he might hurt you?"

She shrugged again. "I dunno. Maybe if he got mad or something. Why are you asking so many questions?"

"Well, I'm concerned about your safety for one."

Becky scoffed at me. "I'm not worried about Brett. I mean, he's creepy, but I stay away from him."

I glanced over at Sammy for reassurance and took a deep breath. "You said he seemed happy about Ms. Underwood's death."

"Yeah, but he's weird like that."

"Do you think he wanted her dead?"

Becky's face brightened into a smile. "Are you going to investigate Ms. Underwood's murder? Are you going to get Mrs. Crowsdale off?"

I held my hands up. "Whoa, whoa, whoa, let's not get ahead of ourselves. I'm just asking you a question."

"You are, aren't you? You don't think Mrs. Crowsdale did it either! Oh my gosh, Fran, thank you so much!" She threw her arms around me.

I looked at Sammy helplessly as I patted Becky on the back. She shrugged uselessly.

"Now, Becky, I don't want you to get your hopes up," I said when she finally let go of me.

"I know you can do it, Fran. You're, like, a murder-solving genius."

I tried to look at Sammy again for help, but she'd abandoned me to go clear a customer's table. I put my hands on Becky's shoulders. "Becky, now listen to me. The police have already investigated Ms. Underwood's murder and made an arrest. Even if I find evidence that someone else could be the murderer, the police may still go forward with their case against Mrs. Crowsdale. I can't make them change their minds. Do you understand?"

"Totally."

I smiled. She understood.

"But I know you can do it. I know you'll prove that she's innocent."

I sighed. Maybe she didn't understand after all. "I'll do my best, but I'm not making any promises."

I kept going before she could assure me yet again that she knew I would exonerate Ann Crowsdale. "Now, do you think it's possible Brett actually wanted Ms. Underwood dead?"

"I mean, yeah, I guess. They got in a fight at practice the other day, and he was calling her a bunch of names and stuff. I thought he was going to hit her, but she got in his face and yelled back, and he eventually just walked out."

"Which day was this?"

"Friday."

"The day she was killed? Did you tell the police?"

"They didn't talk to me." She looked blissfully ignorant of the fact that this was a significant piece of information.

"Who else was there?"

"Everybody. The whole cast, the crew, Mrs. C. It was right out in the open in the auditorium."

If Ann Crowsdale had witnessed the fight, there was no way she wouldn't have told the police. So either they hadn't thought it was important, or they had enough evidence against Ann that it didn't affect their opinion. It could mean that Brett had nothing to do with the murder... or it could mean that the police had just overlooked the lead. And that could mean they had overlooked something else. "You said other kids also seemed happy Ms. Underwood was dead?"

She shrugged. "I mean, yeah, but not as much as Brett."

"Did you ever see Ms. Underwood argue with anyone else?"

"Other than Mrs. Crowsdale? Nope."

I studied her for a minute as I racked my brain for what else to ask her. I could think of only one thing. "Is he online? Can you show me a picture of him?"

"Sure!" She whipped out her phone and tapped on the screen for a few seconds before turning it around to me.

A brown-eyed teenage boy looked back at me. His hair was short and blond. The face he was making in his profile picture was clearly supposed to make him look tough, but the effect was lost on me. Maybe I was getting old.

"May I?" I held out my hand. Becky nodded and passed me the phone. I scrolled down through his posts. It was mostly pictures of him, with or without his friends, but he was making the same tough-guy face in all of them. A few other scattered posts complained about tests or papers, but that was about it.

"Does he bully people online?" I didn't know how to see his activity other than on his own page.

Becky shrugged.

"You don't know, or not really?"

She shrugged again. "I don't see him do it, but that doesn't mean he doesn't do it."

I noticed the blue checkmark at the top of the screen. "You're friends with him."

"Yeah, but that's online. You can't *not* be friends with someone you know."

I thought about all the many people I knew but wasn't friends with online and wondered if I was doing social media wrong. Then I noticed her friend count and realized it was nearly the population of Cape Bay. Not that we lived in a large town, but I still couldn't comprehend how she knew all those people. Although it could be helpful. "What about Ms. Underwood? Are you friends with her?"

Becky made a face as I handed back her phone. "No."

"Oh, I guess you don't friend teachers."

"I do. Just not her." She dropped her phone back in her pocket while I tried to mentally sort out the rules of teenage social media. Your teachers? Sure! A boy your age who you think is weird and creepy and could possibly be capable of murder?

Of course, it would be rude not to! A teacher you don't like? Never!

But I had a feeling that really trying to understand all that would give me a headache, and I had other things to do. "Do you know where Brett would be this time of day? Or where he lives?" I felt creepy asking where a teenage boy lived, but it wasn't like I could just wait for him to wander into the café.

"He lives on my street. Like, directly across the street. I could walk straight out my front door and into his."

Well, that might explain why she was online friends with him. "Do you think he'd be home right now?"

"No." Her tone made me think that she thought I was as old as I felt right about then.

"Do you know where else he could be?" I wished Becky were a little more forthcoming. I felt like I was dragging the information out of her.

"Yeah, he's right over there."

Chapter 9

AFTER I GOT over my embarrassment at talking about the boy when he was practically right next to me, I realized I had a problem. I couldn't exactly walk up to him in the middle of the café and ask him if he killed his teacher. But if I didn't, I'd have to go find him at his house or somewhere else, and that could be complicated.

Before I could decide what to do, he made the decision for me and got up to leave. I had to think fast. I ran to the back and grabbed my purse. For a second, my fingers hovered over the five-dollar bill in my wallet, but then I grabbed the twenty instead. Brett didn't seem like the kind of kid who would be seduced by a mere five dollars.

I dropped my wallet back into my purse, tucked

it away, and headed back out into the café. Brett was gone.

"I'm going to go out for a bit. You guys will be okay without me, right?" I hesitated for a second halfway out the door while I waited for confirmation.

"Yup, we—"

I didn't wait for the rest of Sammy's reply, just pushed the door open and went outside. I instantly realized I should have grabbed my coat, but I'd just have to deal with being cold. I didn't have time to go back to get it and still catch up to Brett.

I looked up and down Main Street for Brett. For a second, I thought he'd disappeared, but then I spotted his white T-shirt and jeans a block away.

"Excuse me! Excuse me! I think you dropped this!" I said, hurrying in his direction. "Excuse me!"

He finally turned around. "I didn't drop anything, lady."

"No, I think you did. It was under your table at the café." I held out the twenty so he could see it.

His eyes lit up. "Oh, yeah. I did. Thanks." He took it from me and stuffed it in his pocket.

"It's Brett, right?" I asked before he could turn around and walk away.

"Who's asking?"

"Me."

He raised his eyebrows.

"Francesca Amaro. I own the café." I gestured behind me like he might confuse us for some other café.

He looked skeptical. "You were at my school the other day."

For a second, I wondered how he knew that before I remembered that he was a student there and must have seen me. Then I realized with a start that I'd seen him too. He was the boy in the principal's office. "Yes, I was. I saw you coming out of the principal's office."

"Yeah. So?"

I shrugged. "I was just saying that I saw you. You're one of Becky's friends, right?" It was an exaggeration, but it served my purposes.

"Yeah, we know each other. What's that got to do with you?"

"Well, I just—" I tried to think of something. "You're in the play together, right? How's that going? It must be really hard right now with one of your directors getting killed and the other one arrested for her murder." It sounded stupid to my ears even as it came out, but I had to get him talking somehow.

He smiled. It was more sneering than happy, though. "Yeah, old Veronica caught it, huh? She had it coming. Too bad about Mrs. C, though. But she's not going to get convicted. She's too nice."

"People don't get acquitted on the basis of being too nice, Brett. They get acquitted because they're innocent."

"Or because there's not enough evidence. Or because everybody hated the lady who got killed and everybody loves the lady on trial."

"I wouldn't want to count on that if I were on trial."

"Well, you're not on trial, are you?" He smirked at me.

"No, fortunately not. But Mrs. Crowsdale is. Do you think she's willing to count on it?"

He shrugged and looked as if he couldn't care less.

"Do you think she did it?"

"Why do you care?"

It was my turn to shrug. "I'm just curious. I don't know either of them, so I don't know what to think."

He looked at me, again seeming to sneer. "Think whatever you want. It doesn't bother me." He turned around to walk away.

"I heard you seemed happy she was dead," I blurted, panicking a little about how to get him to stay.

He turned around slowly. "You did, huh? Who'd you hear that from? Becky?" He took a step closer to me.

I refused to be intimidated, or at least to look that way, and stood my ground. "No, not Becky. It was some other kids."

"Oh yeah?" He took another step closer. "Who were they then?"

I channeled my best tough-girl attitude. "I don't know everybody in this town. They were some high school kids. They were talking in line about how nobody in school was really sad Ms. Underwood was dead but that Brett Wallace actually seemed happy. You're Brett Wallace, aren't you?"

He smirked. "Yeah, I am. And yeah, I'm happy she's dead too. She was a—"

"Enough!" I held my hand up. I could see the word his mouth was starting to form, and I didn't want to hear it. "You know, it's going to make people suspicious if you go around telling people you're happy she's dead. They're going to start thinking the police got the wrong person."

His face darkened. He took another step toward me, getting so close that he could touch me. "Are you saying you think I killed Veronica?"

"I thought you said it didn't bother you what I thought." My heart pounded in my chest. I had met this boy less than five minutes ago, and here I was, accusing him of murder. Well, not in so many words, but that was what he thought I was doing.

"That's right, I don't."

"I was saying that people might think that you killed her if you act happy about it."

"The cops didn't think that."

"You talked to the cops?"

"Is that any of your business?"

I could only think of one reason why it was. "It is if I'm going to help Mrs. Crowsdale."

His eyes narrowed, and he looked me up and down. "I know who you are."

Of course he did. I'd introduced myself.

"You're that lady who solved those murders."

How on earth did he know that? But I took a deep breath. "Yeah, I am."

"So you think the cops screwed up."

"I didn't say that."

"You think the cops screwed up, and you think I killed her. That's why you followed me out here and gave me that twenty."

"You dropped that twenty."

He laughed, but there was no humor in it. "No, I didn't. You said I did so you would have an excuse to talk to me."

He was smarter than I'd expected. I had to figure out a way to get things back on track.

"Didn't expect me to see through your little act, did you?" He took a step toward me. He was uncomfortably close. "I'm not that dumb. Just like I'm not dumb enough to go blabbing about killing Veronica to somebody who's friends with the cops." He smiled a sickening smile. "That wasn't a confession, you know. Or was it? Good luck figuring it out."

A black Mercedes pulled up beside us, and its window rolled down. "Brett, sweetie, it's time to go to your lacrosse lesson," the blond woman inside said.

"Looks like I gotta go." He smirked at me again as he moved toward the car. He pulled the door open and slid inside. As the car started to roll away, he leaned out the window. "Lots of people had reasons to hate Veronica, you know. Not just me."

The car sped away.

I stood there on the sidewalk, staring after it, trying to figure out what to make of Brett. There was something I couldn't quite put my finger on about him. He definitely wanted people to think he was a tough guy, but something about him made me not so sure.

Becky said he grabbed girls, but on the arm.

She didn't want to be alone with him, but she wasn't afraid of him. He insinuated that he killed Veronica Underwood and then got in his mom's car to go to a lacrosse lesson. It was a strange juxtaposition although, I supposed, not completely unheard of. And what was with him calling her by her first name? Was that him trying to be a cool, "rebellious" teenager? Or was there something more to it?

I didn't know, but I would need to find out if I was going to figure out if Brett was the murderer or, for that matter, if it was anyone other than Ann Crowsdale. And to do that, I'd have to see what else I could find out about Brett. And what evidence the police had against Ann.

I realized I was freezing and turned to go back to the café and saw the one person who could help me figure out both of those things. Not that I wanted to talk to him, not about this, anyway. But I wouldn't be able to avoid him. Detective Mike Stanton was walking into my café.

Chapter 10

MIKE SAW me walking toward the café and held the door open for me. "Hey, Franny! How's it going? Aren't you cold out here with no coat on?" He was in an unusually good mood.

"Sure am! But I'm pretty good, Mike. How are you?"

"You know what? I'm doing good. Wouldn't have minded not losing half my weekend to a murder investigation, but at least we got it done without needing to call in civilian help!" He patted me on the back as I walked past him through the door. It almost made me feel bad about what I was going to say next.

"The case has been the talk of the town the past few days. First the murder itself and then Ann

Crowsdale being arrested for it." I took a deep breath, knowing that he probably wouldn't like my next comment, but not feeling that I really had much choice if I was going to get any information out of him. "I'm not sure which people are actually more upset about."

To my surprise, Mike wasn't even fazed. "Yup, Underwood wasn't very popular. I've never seen a person be so universally despised after four months in town."

"She just moved here?" The school secretaries had mentioned that she had just taken over as the drama teacher, but I didn't realize she was new to town too.

"Yup. Moved here from Providence over the summer. Apparently her getting hired on was pretty controversial."

"Really? Why?"

Mike shrugged. "Political school system stuff. She was new to the school, new to the state, comes in and takes over the school's drama department. People weren't happy. That kind of thing happens in law enforcement all the time, but I guess it's a big deal in the school system." He drummed his fingers on the counter and stared up at the menu.

"Are you okay?" I asked. Mike never looked at the menu. Even when he was in a good mood, he just came in and grunted at us, and we gave him large amounts of black coffee.

Mike's forehead wrinkled, and I looked from him to the menu. He broke into a grin. "I'm on my way home. At a normal time for a change. I thought I'd get Sandra something." He stared at the menu for a few more seconds. "What do you think she'd want?"

"Will she want something hot or cold?" I asked as I walked around the counter. I knew I wanted something hot. As soon as I was done helping Mike, I was making myself a hot cappuccino to get the chill out of my bones.

"Something cold." He smiled when I looked at him as if he'd lost his mind. "If I get her something hot, it'll be cold by the time I get it home anyway. May as well get her something that will stay at the right temperature."

Well, at least that made some sense. "Sandra likes herbal tea, right?"

He looked at me blankly.

"Chamomile, rooibos, hibiscus…"

"Those are made-up words."

I shook my head. For a smart man, he had some major blind spots. "We have a new strawberry vanilla tea I bet she'll like. I'll make it extra strong so that it won't get watered down if the ice is melted by the time she gets it."

"Sounds like a plan."

I was proud of our new herbal tea selection. We'd only recently graduated from ancient bags of grocery-store-brand black tea, and I'd put special care into selecting a variety of teas and tea blends to offer our customers. The strawberry was my new favorite. It was surprisingly delicious both hot and cold, though I preferred it cold.

I moved slowly preparing the tea, realizing that this was a prime opportunity to ask Mike some questions without making a big deal out of it.

"People seem really shocked that Ann Crowsdale was arrested," I said as nonchalantly as I could.

"Yeah, well, they wouldn't pay me to investigate crimes if the suspects were always obvious."

"True." I fiddled with the hot water dispenser to buy myself some time. "I guess it was partly how quickly she was arrested that surprised people."

"Most murders are solved quickly. We've just had an unlucky run here lately with cases that weren't so easy."

"It was easy to solve this one?"

"Easier than some cases."

"Well, that's good." I started making Mike's coffee without being asked. I would be stunned if he left my café without a large black coffee in hand even though it was nearly dinnertime. I sometimes suspected that he'd fall asleep instantly without a constant infusion of high doses of caffeine. I was also stalling for time. Mike, being Mike, wasn't volunteering very much information. I started a fresh pot. Mike always liked coffee from a fresh pot. "You must have had some pretty good evidence."

"Enough to make an arrest."

"Everybody seems to think so highly of Ann. They're really having trouble believing that she could have murdered someone." I was fiddling with our cups and saucers while I waited for Mike's coffee to brew but glanced over at him just in time to see him narrow his eyes at me.

"What are you getting at, Fran?" He was suddenly using his stern cop voice instead of his genial old-friend voice.

I sighed and rested my hands on the counter. "Do you ever wonder if you made a mistake, Mike? If you got the wrong person? I'm not saying you did, but when you arrest someone as universally loved as Ann for something as awful as murder, do you ever wonder if you got it wrong?"

For a very long, very uncomfortable moment, he didn't say anything. I felt the way I imagined suspects felt when he was interrogating them—very on the spot, very scrutinized, very judged. And then Mike's face softened.

"Yeah. Yeah, I do. If the evidence had pointed to anyone but Ann, I would have been more than happy to follow it as far as I could." He shook his head. "Sandra and Ann have been on the PTA together at the kids' school for years, and Sandra can't say enough good things about her. I would love to be wrong on this one. But the evidence—the evidence is too strong to ignore."

Mike's coffee was ready, so I filled our biggest to-go cup to the brim and put the lid on. "Be careful. It's hot."

"Do I owe you for Sandra's drink?"

"Nope. Police and fire eat and drink free." It had been our café's policy since my grandparents' era.

"Wives count?"

"At least when you're ordering for her."

Mike grinned. "What about cookies for the kids?"

"You're pushing it, Stanton," I said with false annoyance. I filled up a bag with cookies anyway, including some I knew Mike and Sandra would like more than the kids.

"Thanks, Franny. See you tomorrow. And Merry Christmas!"

"Merry Christmas!" I called back as he made his way to the door.

"Merry Christmas, Mike!" Sammy said, emerging from the back room with her coat on.

Mike waved and returned the good wishes before he went out the door.

"Headed out?" I asked Sammy.

"Yup."

Before either of us could say anything, a woman with bleached blond hair walked up to the counter. "Excuse me." She smiled. "It's Sammy, right?"

Sammy nodded.

The woman smiled bigger and stuck her hand out. "I'm Cheryl."

"Hi, Cheryl," Sammy said, shaking her hand. "Is there anything I can help you with?"

"No," the woman said, still smiling. "I just wanted to introduce myself." She turned around and walked out of the café. Sammy and I stared after her.

"Do you know her?" I asked after a few seconds.

"No," Sammy said slowly. "But now that I think about it, she's been here almost the whole day."

I thought back and realized that she had been lurking in one of the corners of the café most of the day. We had a few people who did that—spending hours hiding behind a laptop or lost in a book—so I hadn't really thought much of it. As long as we weren't so busy that we didn't have any open tables, I never minded people setting up camp for the day. It was mostly locals who did it, but even during the off-season, we had a few tourists who would spend the day using our free Wi-Fi or enjoying one of our comfy chairs, so I hadn't thought much of the fact that I didn't recognize the woman.

"How did she know my name?" Sammy asked.

I shrugged. "Maybe she overheard it?"

"Maybe." Sammy stared at the door. It was late enough in the year that the street was already dark.

"Do you want to call Ryan to walk you home?"

Sammy stared for a few more seconds then shook her head. "What would I tell him? Some lady introduced herself to me, and now I'm scared?"

I had to admit it didn't sound like a particularly scary encounter. But there had definitely been something odd about it.

"Besides, he doesn't get off work for another couple of hours."

I wanted to argue back that escorting an anxious citizen home seemed well within the bounds of on-duty police officer activities, but I knew it wouldn't make any difference.

Sammy took a deep breath and straightened her shoulders. "I'll be fine. She's just a strange woman.

There's nothing to be afraid of. I'll see you tomorrow, Fran. Have a good night."

"Good night, Sammy," I replied as she walked toward the door. Just before she pushed it open, I called out something else: "Call me when you get home."

Chapter 11

SAMMY MADE it home safely and without anything else odd happening, but I still felt uneasy walking home myself. Fortunately, Matt and Latte met me halfway and walked me the rest of the way back to Matt's house, where he had his specialty, spaghetti Bolognese, waiting for us. He'd learned to make polenta with shrimp on our Italian vacation, bringing his repertoire up to two whole dishes, but spaghetti with meat sauce was still his go-to meal.

"So what's on your mind?" Matt asked as I sat at the dinner table while he put the finishing touches on our dinner.

"Nothing, really." I scratched Latte's head where it rested on my knee. With the other hand, I sipped from the generous glass of red wine beside my plate.

"Nothing?"

I looked up to see Matt looking at me incredulously instead of stirring the sauce as he should have been. "What?"

"You've barely said two words to me. Either you've got something on your mind, or you're mad at me for some reason. It's not the spaghetti, is it? I thought about making polenta, but I've made it so many times since we got back from Italy——"

"I'm not mad at you," I said, cutting him off. I chose not to point out that the "so many times" he'd made polenta was actually only two. "I guess I've just been thinking."

"About?"

I sighed.

"You've been thinking about investigating that murder, haven't you?"

I nodded and made kissy faces at Latte.

"Have you already started?"

I scratched Latte's head some more.

"Franny?"

I sighed again and turned around so I was looking at him. Latte wandered off to find one of his chew toys. "Yes, I already started."

"And?"

I took a deep breath and let it out slowly. "I don't know."

He was still staring at me, his back to the bubbling pot of sauce.

"You're going to get sauce on your jersey."

He jumped away from the stove as though I'd told him he was on fire. A stain on his beloved New England Patriots football jersey would be earth shattering. He stripped it off, folded it neatly, and laid it over a chair. Unfortunately, he had a long-sleeved T-shirt on underneath it. Fortunately, it was a thermal shirt and on the snug side.

Matt turned back to the stove and scooped a big pile of spaghetti onto each of our plates and then topped it with a generous ladleful of Bolognese sauce. My grandmother would have rolled over in her grave to see the sauce just dumped on top like that instead of being mixed in with the pasta, but I wasn't going to complain about details when I had a good-looking man making me dinner.

He brought the plates over to the table and set them down then went back to pull the garlic bread out of the oven. My mouth watered at the smell of it. He brought it over to the table and sat down then waited until I had put the first bite in my mouth to start back up with the questions.

"You said you don't know about the investigation. What don't you know?"

I swallowed my spaghetti. "This is really good, by the way."

"Franny."

I heaved a sigh and put my fork down. At least I knew there was plenty more on the stove if mine got cold. I started by telling him about the Crowsdales' visit to the café and my talk with Becky then about my chat with Brett.

"Wait, you followed a teenage boy out of Antonia's to ask him if he murdered his teacher?" he asked around a mouthful of spaghetti.

I stared at him for a second. "Well, when you put it that way, it sounds creepy."

Matt laughed. Thankfully, he'd swallowed his food first. "Yeah, it kind of does, Franny."

"If anything, he's the creepy one," I retorted, realizing full well how weak a defense it sounded.

He laughed again. "So do you think he did it?"

I groaned and shifted in my seat. I grabbed a piece of garlic bread from the plate, tore off a piece, and stuffed it in my mouth. Finally, I answered. "That's what I don't really know. Part of me thinks yes. He argued with her, he obviously hated her, and Becky said he gets aggressive. She clearly thinks he's capable of it. But something about him…" I tore off another piece of garlic bread and thought while I chewed it. "Either he did it, or he likes people thinking he could have."

"Hmm."

I wasn't sure if Matt was thinking or just completely engrossed in eating. "Have the police talked to him? Since you said he got in a shouting match with her?"

"That's the thing—they have. And they still arrested Ann Crowsdale. So maybe I'm wrong? But they arrested her so quickly. You know, Mike came into the café today—"

"You must have been shocked," Matt interrupted. Mike's coffee habit was a well-known fact.

"Oh, I was," I deadpanned back before giving him the highlights of my talk with Mike, including how sure he seemed of his arrest despite the public's shock.

"You know," he said when I was done, "I feel kind of bad for the guy. He takes a few days to solve a murder—"

I cleared my throat.

"With some help from his friendly local coffee dealer. But the town's all over him to hurry it up and get it solved. He makes a quick arrest, and the town's all over him for getting the wrong person. The poor guy catches hell no matter what he does."

I thought about it. It was true. No matter what Mike did, people were on his case about it. It was the trouble with a small town. Everybody knew everything about everybody and had an opinion about them. And that opinion could very well change from minute to minute depending on which way the wind was blowing.

"What time is it?" Matt asked all of a sudden.

I shrugged.

He turned around and looked at the clock on the stove. "The game's about to start! Do you mind if we finish dinner in the living room?"

He was already standing up with his plate before I could even start to open my mouth to give an answer. But it was fine. I needed some time to think, anyway, and "watching" the football game would give me that opportunity. I sure wasn't going to be following the plays.

Matt disappeared into the living room, and I got up to follow.

"Hey, you forgot to put your jersey back on," I said, noticing it still draped over the chair where he'd left it. I picked it up and carried it into the living room with me.

Matt was frozen with the remote in his hand, and I saw him look from the jersey in my hand to the bowl of spaghetti in his and back again. I could practically see his mental anguish as he weighed the dangers of getting Bolognese sauce on his jersey against the bad luck of not wearing it while his beloved Patriots played.

"How about we put it on the couch behind you so you're still touching it, but you won't have to worry about getting sauce on it?" I suggested.

He hesitated. Apparently touching it didn't equate to having it actually on his body.

I decided to have mercy on him. "If you get sauce on it, I can probably get the stain out."

A smile spread across his face. "Really?"

"I can try. Or, you know, we could always put a bib on you," I joked.

"Good idea!" He put his spaghetti down on the coffee table and literally ran into his bedroom as I stared after him in shock. He came back out a moment later with an old, paint-spattered shirt in his hand. He took his jersey from me, put it on, and then tucked the T-shirt all around his neckline. He looked incredibly silly, but he clearly didn't mind. He plopped down on the couch, turned on the game, picked up his spaghetti, and dug back into it.

I just shook my head and sat down next to him with my legs tucked under me. As though he could sense that I was now in a position that allowed for cuddling, Latte appeared, chewy in mouth, from

Matt's room, where he liked to lie on the bed, and jumped on the couch next to me, resting his head on my knee.

I ate my spaghetti and thought about the case while Matt cheered on his team. I really didn't know if there even was a case. And I felt bad for Mike. He couldn't win no matter what he did. He was damned if he did and damned if he didn't. I wondered what the repercussions would be for him if I found enough evidence to show that Ann Crowsdale hadn't been the one to kill Veronica Underwood—that it had been Brett Wallace or maybe someone else I hadn't thought of yet. Not that the repercussions for Mike mattered more than preventing an innocent woman from going to jail.

On the other hand, I might find evidence to bolster his case or to help the public see that he was right. As much as I'd liked Ann when I met her, she deserved to go to jail if she was guilty. And that could shore up Mike's reputation. But Sammy and Becky would be devastated. I imagined I felt a little bit like Mike must feel.

I decided to talk to Rhonda the next day. Her boys went to Cape Bay High. She was involved with the school. Maybe she'd have some insight into the case.

I took another bite of spaghetti, finding myself

a little frustrated that there wasn't really anything else I could do about the case until the next day.

"Do you need more spaghetti?" Matt asked, standing up.

I looked up at him, confused. He never got up while the game was on. And then I realized it had gone to commercial. And that commercial was for the social network that Becky had shown me Brett's profile on earlier. And all of a sudden, I realized there was something I could do on the case that night. I could find Veronica Underwood's profile and see what she'd been up to online.

Chapter 12

I BORROWED Matt's laptop and settled in with a fresh glass of wine to spend the rest of the game digging around online for information about Veronica Underwood. She was on all the usual social networks, the ones I knew how to use, anyway —I skipped the one that only people under twenty-five seem to use. I scanned through her profile on the professional social network first. I didn't expect to find anything useful there, but I thought it might give me a little insight into her.

It didn't. The profile was sparsely populated, with only three connections, no college listed, and what I assumed had to be her previous job the only one listed.

That reminded me that I hadn't updated my

profile on that network since I'd moved back to Cape Bay. It still listed me as working at the PR job I'd left over the summer. I took a few minutes to update it, changing my old job to actually show as my old job and adding Antonia's in at the top. It felt strange typing in that I was the owner. I'd said it what felt like a million times over the previous six months or so, but seeing it in black and white on the screen felt wrong. It should be my grandparents' café. Or my mother's. But mine alone? It felt as if I was lying to the world.

Before I could slip into nostalgia that would surely be accompanied by tears, I moved on to the next site. Nothing much useful there. Just pictures of Veronica and her food and some sunsets with inspirational quotes. I started to scan through the people she followed, but quickly gave up. There were too many of them, and without real names, I couldn't even begin to make sense of whether they were useful suspects.

The next site was more of the same—some quotes, a lot of sharing of other people's posts, some conversations between her and some other people that I could barely follow. Nothing blared "My murderer is Brett Wallace!" or "My murderer is Ann Crowsdale!" I gave the list of people she was following a cursory glance but found it no more useful than I had the previous social site.

I finally made my way to the site Becky had used earlier to show me Brett's picture. Veronica's profile was easy to find. I scrolled through the posts on her page. It appeared to be all of them. Somebody hadn't been up to date on her privacy settings. Something seemed strange about them beyond the fact that they appeared to all be visible, but I couldn't quite place what it was. They all seemed normal and innocuous, if a little abrasive. She did seem to get annoyed with lots of businesses and strangers she ran into on the street and didn't seem to hesitate to share that with the world. Still, it was nothing that seemed worth killing her over and nothing to indicate who her murderer was.

I flipped over to the list of her friends. I wasn't sure if it was strange that we had none in common. In a small town like Cape Bay, everyone pretty much knew everyone else, but between her being new in town and me only recently having returned to town, I decided it probably wasn't significant. What was significant were some of the names that showed up on her list, especially compared to the names that weren't there. No Becky, as I expected, or Amanda, my other part-time high schooler. No Ann Crowsdale. In fact, I didn't see any other employees of the school, except for Marcus Varros, the principal. And while there were a few people who looked like teenagers, the only one I found who lived in Cape Bay was a blond-haired boy with a sneer. Brett Wallace.

I clicked over to his page. It was much more locked down. All I could see were his old profile pictures, which were all variations on a theme. Boy making tough-guy face in different settings, sometimes with friends. It almost reminded me of Monet's water lilies paintings—same subject, different lighting and locations—except much less poetic. It occurred to me that maybe I'd had too much wine.

Deciding that there wasn't much more to glean from Brett's profile, I closed the laptop and cuddled up to Matt to think about the case until the game was over. The TV screen claimed there were only twelve minutes left, but I knew that meant there were at least thirty. The Patriots were winning comfortably, but Matt wouldn't get up until the game was completely over. My eyes felt heavy from the combination of wine and good food and a busy day at the café.

"Franny, come on, let's go to bed."

"What?" I tried to open my eyes, but they didn't

want to. That was fine. I was comfortable where I was.

"Franny." Matt rubbed my leg vigorously as he singsonged my name.

"Mmmm." I nestled deeper into his shoulder.

"All right, Franny."

I slid down onto the couch as Matt moved out from under me. That was fine too. The couch was comfortable.

Matt grunted as he pushed his hands under me and tried to lift me. That was not comfortable.

I sat up. "Okay, okay, I'll get up."

"Good, because I don't think my back could take it."

"Hey!" I swatted at him as I got myself to my feet. He just laughed. Halfway to the bedroom, I stopped. "I know what it is!"

"What? You know who killed that teacher?"

"No!" I turned around and laid my hands on his chest, momentarily distracting myself with the feel of his muscles under his shirt. He'd been going to the gym, and it was paying off.

"Then what?" He slid his arms around my waist and pulled me closer to him.

"What was weird about her profile page!"

Matt raised an eyebrow but tipped his head down to kiss me. If I'd been more awake, I probably would have thought that he wasn't as interested in what I had figured out as he was about other things.

"Have you ever had a friend die?"

"What?" He pulled away from me, looking at me as if I was crazy.

"Online! Have you ever seen what happens to someone's profile page when they die?"

"No?"

"Or when your dad died! What did people post on your page?"

"Condolences?"

"Yes! Exactly! Condolences! When people die, their pages get flooded with condolences! Everyone shares memories, talks about what a tragedy it is, says they can't believe they're gone."

"Okay. And? What does that have to do with that teacher?"

"There was none of that on her page! No one posted about how upset they were! It was like no one cared at all!"

Matt's face flickered in something like confusion. "You're excited about that?"

I realized how awful I sounded. "Well, no, I'm not excited. I'm not happy about someone being so universally disliked that no one seems to care that she died. But it may mean that there are more people who actually did dislike her enough that they wanted her dead."

"It's a long way from disliking someone to wanting them dead. Especially wanting them dead enough to kill them."

I sighed. He was right. I hated when he was right. Especially when it meant that I was wrong. Not that I was really wrong about it. Just that the lack of condolences on her page really only confirmed what I already knew—that people didn't like her. It didn't tell me that people were happy that she was dead or that they actually wanted to kill her. More importantly, it didn't tell me *who* might have wanted her dead.

"You're mad that I'm right, aren't you?" Matt wrapped his arms around me and pulled me close to him again.

I shrugged.

"Can I make it up to you?"

"Maybe."

"How's this?" He leaned in and kissed me, the kind of kiss that made my toes curl at the same time as it made me want to melt into him.

"It's a start."

He smiled and kissed me again.

Later that night, I lay awake, staring at the ceiling. I wasn't the slightest bit tired. Apparently my nap at the end of the game had made my body think I didn't need to really go to sleep for a few more hours. I used the time to think about Veronica Underwood and Ann Crowsdale and Brett Wallace. Veronica, by all accounts, had been a miserable person, but I didn't think Ann had killed her. She just didn't seem capable of it. And Brett. Brett I didn't know about. He was either capable of murder or very determined to have people think he was. It was strange. I couldn't imagine why someone would *want* people to think they could be a murderer. Especially not someone so young. What would make a teenage boy want people to think he was capable of murder? Or worse, what would make a teenage boy actually be capable of murder? Or commit it?

I wasn't sure whether the wind from outside had found its way in through the poorly insulated areas around the windows or if it was the result of thinking about such a grim subject, but I felt a sudden chill and pulled the blankets tighter around me.

Chapter 13

RHONDA WAS WORKING the next morning when I got to the café. I was glad, because I had some questions I wanted to ask her. Namely, what she knew about Brett Wallace and anyone else at the school that might have had a grudge against Veronica Underwood.

"Brett?" She laughed. "I've known him since he was three years old. He went to preschool with my oldest."

"So you know him pretty well?"

"Not as well as some of the other kids, but yeah, I know him fairly well."

I took a deep breath. I was afraid to offend her with my next question. Not that Rhonda was easily offended, but I wasn't usually asking about a teenager's capacity for murder. "Does he seem—" I stopped to search for the right word "—odd to you?"

"Brett?" She laughed again. "He's not as odd as he wants people to think."

"What do you mean?"

"Back when the kids first started grade school, he was having some behavior problems, so his parents and the school had him tested for every learning disability in the book. Dyslexia, ADD, ADHD. I'm pretty sure they even screened him for autism, just in case. But everything came back negative. Eventually, they gave him an IQ test, thinking that maybe he had a very low IQ despite hitting all his milestones." She gave me a meaningful look that I couldn't understand the meaning of.

"So did he?"

"Off the charts."

"Ohh." I thought back over my interaction with Brett and tried to think of whether an intellectual disability changed the meaning of anything he said.

"The other way, Fran."

I looked at her for a second, trying to figure out what she meant. Then it dawned on me. "He's a genius."

Rhonda nodded. "Highest IQ his evaluator had ever seen. So they had him retested, because it couldn't possibly be that high, right? Nope. Three times, they had him tested, including by the top child psychologist up in Boston. Astronomical IQ. The kid's a literal genius."

"So why is he at Cape Bay High? It's not a bad school, but—" I thought a kid like that would probably be more challenged in one of the many highly competitive private schools in the area. Parents in California sent their kids to them, they were so good.

"He didn't want to go somewhere else."

"He didn't want to?"

"They've tried to move him a bunch of times, but he fails out every time."

"How?"

"He sleeps. In all his classes. Never does the work. He does that at Cape Bay High too, but his test scores make up for it."

"He actually takes the tests?" This kid was baffling.

"Oh, yeah. He doesn't want to fail out of there. My son has chemistry with him this year, and he told me Brett's corrected the teacher's formulas a couple of times. Head on his desk, looks like he's sound asleep, and just pipes up and points out the errors in his formulas then goes back to sleep."

I'd heard of genius kids being troublemakers

before, but people always chalked it up to them not being challenged enough. It sounded as if Brett didn't want to be challenged, though. He just wanted to intimidate people. "So what's with the tough-guy act?"

Rhonda shrugged. "It's been going on for a couple of years now. I think it's a fun new game for him to see how he can manipulate people by being threatening."

"Do you think he would ever actually hurt someone?"

Rhonda's eyes narrowed. For a second, I thought she was angry, but then her face lit up a little. "Do you think he had something to do with Veronica Underwood's murder?"

I shrugged. "His name came up. Apparently he argued with her the day she died."

Rhonda crossed her arms and thought for a few seconds. "You know, I don't really know. Part of me says he's a nice boy who just wants to be misunderstood, but another part of me…" She trailed off, but I could tell she was still thinking. "Another part of me could see the tough-guy thing not being an act after all. Maybe he thinks it's fun to intimidate people, and if that's the case, I could see where he might take that too far."

A chill ran down my spine. She'd said almost

exactly what I was thinking, but it was still unsettling to hear it said out loud, especially in Rhonda's matter-of-fact tone.

She continued, "I'd like to think that's not the case, but you never can tell, I guess."

That answer didn't exactly give me much reassurance. I decided to move on. "You know the school pretty well. Do you know anyone else who might want to hurt her?"

She practically snorted. "Want to? Everyone! You met her, didn't you?"

"Well, yeah."

"So you know what I mean. No one liked her."

"Did anyone dislike her enough to want her dead?"

She gave me a pointed look. "I'm going to assume you mean whether someone hated her enough to go out of their way to kill her. Because I think we already know that people aren't too torn up about her death."

"Well, there's a difference between not being upset about it and actually wanting her dead," I said, finding myself echoing Matt's words from the night before.

"True. But to answer your question, I don't know. I know more about the school from the parent side than the personnel side. If someone had a grudge against her, I wouldn't know about it unless it was so bad that the kids found out."

I sighed. I'd hoped Rhonda would be a veritable font of information, virtually laying the case out in front of me. But it couldn't be that easy, could it?

"You could always call the school, talk to Principal Varros. I don't know if he'd tell you anything, but it can't hurt to try, can it?"

I agreed it couldn't. And I didn't really have any other leads to follow. Besides, maybe he could give me some more insight into Brett.

I let Rhonda get back to work and sat down at the computer to pull up the school's number. Searching for Cape Bay High School of course returned several articles about the murder, just as searching for Veronica Underwood's name the night before had. It had been big news over the weekend—teacher found dead in school parking lot. It was the kind of thing local news channels and newspapers lived for.

I found the number and dialed it on the café's phone.

"Thank you for calling Cape Bay High School. This is Marian Bayless. How may I help you this morning?"

I'd only planned to ask to be transferred to Principal Varros, but hearing Mrs. Bayless's voice on the line gave me an idea.

"Hi, Mrs. Bayless, this is Francesca Amaro—"

"Franny! How are you?"

"I'm good, Mrs. Bayless. How are you?"

"Oh, I'm getting by. I'm getting by. It was so nice to see you the other day. Terrible about Veronica, though. That was who you were here to see, wasn't it?"

"Yes. Mrs. Bayless—"

"It's horrible for the children to be exposed to such a thing. Although with Veronica's attitude, she —well, I shouldn't speak ill of the dead. So what can I help you with, dear?"

"Mrs. Bayless, I was wondering if you and Mrs. Crawford would like to come over to Antonia's after school and have coffee with me. My treat, of course."

"Oh, Franny, that would be lovely! We both enjoyed your visit the other day, and it would be so nice to get to spend some more time catching up with you."

I didn't want to tell her that I really just wanted to find out what they knew about Veronica Underwood and who might have had it in for her. As the school secretaries, they would be privy to almost all the goings-on of the school, including any interpersonal conflicts Veronica Underwood might have had with other members of the staff. I couldn't be sure that they'd be willing to share any of that information, but they seemed to like me, so I had some hope.

I also hoped to get their impressions of Brett Wallace.

"So we'll see you this afternoon then, Franny?"

"Yes. If I'm not out front, just ask for me."

She started to get off the phone, but I remembered that I hadn't accomplished my main goal in calling the school. "Actually, Mrs. Bayless, I have one more thing."

"Oh, of course, Franny. What else can I do for you?"

"Is Principal Varros in? Could I speak with him?"

There was a pause that I didn't know whether to chalk up to her checking on whether he was available or her being suspicious of my question.

"He's busy right now, dear, but if you'd like to come in, I can set a meeting up for you tomorrow morning."

I didn't want to wait that long, but unless I was going to go lurk outside the school to wait for him to leave, I didn't have much choice. "Sure, that'll be great."

"And what would you like to discuss with him, dear?"

I couldn't very well tell her I wanted to ply him for information about potential murderers on his staff, so I came up with a quick, plausible lie. "Well, as you know, before her death, Veronica and I had an agreement for Antonia's to sell some baked goods at the play. Now that she and Ann Crowsdale, um—" Thankfully, Mrs. Bayless cut me off.

"Oh, Gwen Blarney's directing the play now. Do you want me to set you up with her instead?"

A new director! I hadn't thought about that. I thought fast. "Well, um, it's a matter of the payment."

"Oh! I didn't realize the food wasn't being donated!"

Did I hear judgment in her voice? I couldn't worry about that now. "It is, but for tax purposes, I need some papers signed. I was supposed to get them to Veronica to have Principal Varros sign, but well—it'll probably just be easier for me to go straight to him than to have to go over it all with the new director."

"Gwen Blarney," she repeated. "But yes, I suppose you're right. Gwen has quite a lot on her plate right now, what with jumping into the play right before it opens and all. It probably will just be easier for you to go straight to Marcus."

I breathed a sigh of relief. I had my meeting with Varros. Now I just had to work up some official-looking papers for him to sign so my cover wouldn't be totally blown.

We confirmed the appointment for first thing the next morning and said our goodbyes. I had just hung up the phone when I heard a loud, angry voice coming from the café.

"Where's Francesca? I need to talk to her! Now!" The voice was Mike Stanton's, and if he was using my full name, I knew I was in trouble.

Chapter 14

I THOUGHT about running out the back door, but Mike was standing at the door to the café's back room before I could even get out of my chair. I was pretty sure I'd never seen him so angry.

"Just what in the hell do you think you're doing, Francesca?" he yelled.

Trying to figure out how to escape. I thought it but knew it was probably unwise to say out loud. I took a deep breath and tried to think clearly. "Why don't you close the door, Mike?"

"You're damn right, I'll close the door!" He slammed the door behind him as he stalked over to me. As loud as he was, I didn't think the door being closed would make much of a difference, but at least I could pretend it would. "You're lucky I don't drag you down to the station!"

I stood up so I didn't feel quite so much like he was towering over me. "Now, Mike, just take a deep breath, and we'll sort out whatever this is like adults."

"Sit down! Or I *will* take you down to the station!"

I sat.

"Now *what* in the *hell* do you think you're doing?"

I tried to swallow, but my throat was entirely dry.

"Answer me!" He slammed his hand down on the desk so hard I jumped.

"What do you mean?" My voice came out as barely more than a strangled whisper.

The door to the café cracked open, and Sammy stuck her head in. "Is everything—"

"Get out, Sammy!"

The door quickly closed.

Mike turned back to me. "Now answer me, dammit! What the hell are you doing?"

"I really don't know what you mean." At the moment, I really didn't. I hadn't been yelled at since, well, since my old boss found out I had refused to issue a statement on behalf of one of our movie star PR clients about how it wasn't his fault he'd hit his wife so hard she got a concussion. I hadn't been able to think clearly that time either.

"Yes, you do, Francesca." Mike's voice dropped to a growl, which was somehow even scarier than him yelling.

I fought to think clearly.

"You're really going to play dumb with me, Francesca?" He loomed over me. "You need me to *tell* you?"

I wasn't sure if I actually managed to nod or just quivered in a way that looked like one, but either way, he seemed to take it as a yes.

"You're ruining a kid's life, Francesca, that's what you're doing!"

I stared at him blankly.

"You're so wrapped up in your little game, you don't even realize it, do you? Well, I do. And my boss does. It would be hard not to when Brett Wallace's mother is calling his office complaining that you're going around town slandering her little boy by accusing him of committing a murder that's already been *solved*!"

Brett. Brett, of course. Brett the literal genius. Brett's mother with the honey-blond hair that had to cost a pretty penny to keep up, who drove around Cape Bay in her shiny new black Mercedes. Of course. Of course she would call the police. Of course.

"But—but how—" I could barely stammer out the few words.

"You haven't been very subtle about it, have you, Francesca?"

I was starting to wonder if using my full name was some kind of interrogation technique that was meant to try to intimidate me. Or possibly to distance himself from me. If it was the former, it was working. If it was the latter, well, I wasn't the one who would know.

"Talking about it openly in the café. Tracking him down on the street and trying to *bribe* him to talk to you. Did you really think no one would notice?"

I was starting to regain my composure. And no, I really didn't think anyone would notice. Becky and I had spoken quietly. Rhonda and I had talked in the back room. No one had been around when I talked to Brett on the street except his mother when she picked him up. And the only way she could have known about the money was if he told her. And of course he did. It was the perfect way to manipulate me into backing off the case. Backing off my investigation into *him* being the one who actually murdered Veronica Underwood.

"I—I'm sorry, Mike, I—"

"Don't apologize to me, Fran. I don't want to hear it." Some of the heat had gone out of his voice, but I could tell he was still angry. "You know what pisses me off maybe even more than you screwing around with the Wallace kid's life? The fact that you don't trust my judgment. I told you we had good evidence against Ann Crowsdale, but do you care? No. Why? Because she seems nice. I've spent the last fifteen years of my life investigating crimes and criminals, but you think she's nice, so that counts more in your book. Well, you know what counts more in my book? Evidence! Evidence, Fran! Video evidence counts more in my book than any amount of thinking someone is nice!"

"You have video evidence?"

"Yeah, we do. But you didn't know that, did you? No, of course not, because you're *not a cop*. You're a civilian. And do you know who investigates murders? Cops. Not civilians. At least that's the way it worked until you came waltzing back into town, thinking that you know everything because you spent some time in the big city. Well, you know what, Fran? You don't know everything. Not about crime, not about murders, and you sure as hell don't know everything about this case!"

They had video evidence. I didn't know that. I

couldn't get it out of my head. They had video evidence. That meant she did it. Of course it did. How could it mean anything but? My mind was reeling.

And video evidence meant that Brett wasn't the murderer. He couldn't be. He wasn't manipulating me. He really was a scared kid who had gone to his mom for help. There was no ulterior motive. I was an adult bullying a kid about a crime he didn't commit. I was a bad person.

I sat in the chair, stunned.

"You don't have anything to say for yourself?" Mike asked.

For a few seconds, I opened and closed my mouth like a fish out of water as I tried to figure out what to say.

"We were friends, Fran. Before you left, after you came back. We were friends. You know my wife, my kids. I stood here in this café not even twenty-four hours ago and told you that the evidence overwhelmingly pointed to Ann Crowsdale, and you still went behind my back, looking for someone else, anyone else who could have done it. And who did you pick? A kid! You can't even pick on someone your own size." He stared down at me and shook his head. I didn't recognize the look in his eyes. He didn't look at me like a friend. "You should be ashamed of yourself."

He turned on his heel and left, slamming the door behind him.

I sat in my chair, unmoving.

The door opened again. I braced for Mike to yell at me some more. But it wasn't Mike.

"Franny?" Sammy slipped in and closed the door behind her. "Oh my God, Franny! Are you okay?"

I looked up at her concern-filled face.

"You're crying!"

Was I? I swiped at one of my cheeks and looked at my hand. It was wet. "I didn't realize."

"Oh, Franny—" Sammy leaned down and gave me a hug. "Are you okay?"

I nodded and swiped at my other cheek then ran my fingers under my eyes to get rid of the mascara I knew was pooled there. Sure enough, my fingers came away with black smudges on them.

Sammy smiled.

"It didn't help," I said.

"No. It's sort of worse. It's all—" She gestured broadly across her cheeks. "You look like a baseball player with that black stuff under their eyes."

I tried to laugh, but it came out sounding more like a sob. Sammy hugged me again.

The door opened, and Rhonda poked her head in. "I'm sorry, but Sammy, could you come help me? The book club just got here."

"Of course, I'll be right there."

"Are you okay, Fran?" Rhonda asked.

I nodded. She gave me a sympathetic smile and disappeared back out into the café.

"Are you sure you're okay?" Sammy asked.

I nodded again. "I just need a few minutes."

"Of course," Sammy said. She went back out into the café to help deal with rearranging the tables and chairs and filling the food and drink orders for the book club. It was always an ordeal. Not that I complained, because they were good regular customers, and they spent a lot. I knew I should be out there to help, but I needed a minute.

I felt awful. About Brett, yes, but more than that, about Mike. The way he looked at me—as if I were someone he didn't know but didn't particularly think he liked. And he had been my friend.

I sat there for a few more minutes then got up and pulled out a makeup mirror to try and make myself presentable. When I was satisfied that I looked more presentable than not, I went back out into the café to make myself useful.

It turned out they didn't really need me. Sammy and Rhonda had gotten the book clubbers all arranged and settled with their fancy, foamy, highly sweetened drinks and a pile of cookies in the middle of the table.

I looked around for something that needed to be done, and my eyes landed on a large to-go cup. "Whose is this?" I asked. I wanted to think that whomever they'd prepared it for had just gone to the restroom, but I was afraid it had been sitting there for a while and they'd forgotten to deliver it. Rhonda and Sammy exchanged a look that made me think it was the latter. I picked it up to feel the temperature. It was cool enough that it was clearly not fresh. I opened my mouth to say that they needed to make whoever it was another cup, but Rhonda stopped me.

"It was for Mike. He said he didn't want it."

Chapter 15

I STOOD THERE, holding Mike's abandoned coffee cup, and tried to process the fact that my coffee-mainlining friend had, for the first time ever, left without a cup of coffee in his hand. I had screwed up worse than I thought.

I was so absorbed in my mistake that I didn't even hear the bell over the café door jingle.

"Sammy! Are you okay? What's going on?"

I looked up to see Ryan practically running over to Sammy.

"I'm fine. It's okay. It's over," she said as he pulled her into his arms. I had never seen them so openly affectionate before.

"What happened?" he asked, holding onto her shoulders but stepping back a little from her so he could see her face. "You didn't get robbed, did you?"

She shook her head then looked over at me.

I suddenly had a feeling I knew why Ryan was there. So then I was embarrassed on top of feeling bad about Brett and Mike.

Sammy must have taken my lack of protest as agreement, because she turned back to Ryan. "Mike was here, and he was yelling at Fran. I didn't know what to do, so I called you to see if you could come calm him down."

Ryan exhaled a sigh of relief and closed his eyes for just a second. Opening them again, he said, "Yeah, I heard that he was on the warpath." He turned to me. "You all right, Fran? You know Mike's bark is worse than his bite."

I nodded. It wasn't Mike's bark or his bite that I was afraid of, although I would be pretty scared if he actually tried to bite me for some reason. What I was actually afraid of was losing him as a friend. And that ship might have already sailed.

"The chief was pretty mad when that lady called in. He tore into Mike about it, and I guess that's why Mike tore into you. Crap rolls downhill, you know?"

I knew. What I didn't know was whether to feel honored or offended that I was apparently at the bottom of the police department's hierarchy of yelling.

"I'm sure he didn't mean to make you upset or anything."

I begged to differ, but it didn't seem worth getting into a whole conversation with Ryan about it.

"He'll probably be back in an hour to get another cup of coffee."

I looked down at the full cup of coffee in my hand. I wasn't sure Ryan was right.

Ryan must have run out of things to say, or else my continued silence finally put him off. Not that I was trying to, but I really couldn't muster up anything to say that wouldn't make me sound like a reprimanded child. He looked at Sammy helplessly.

She patted his arm and smiled over at me. "Have you placed that napkin order yet?"

I wrinkled my forehead in confusion. We'd gotten two boxes of napkins in the day before. She'd unpacked them herself.

"Rhonda and I will be fine out here if you need to go in the back for a few minutes. To work on the order."

I realized what she was doing. She was giving me an excuse to go hide for a few more minutes until I could get over my combined embarrassment and dismay. I nodded. "Good idea." I put Mike's abandoned coffee down on the counter and turned to go to the back room to be alone for a few minutes while I regained my composure.

"You forgot your coffee," Ryan said.

For a second, Sammy and I locked eyes. I could see her silent question—did I want her to correct Ryan? I didn't. I picked the cup back up. "Thanks," I said to him. I headed for the back room but was stopped short again by Ryan's voice, this time coming harshly behind me.

"What are you doing here?" He sounded angry.

I turned around to see who he was talking to. He was glaring into the back corner of the café. I looked over and saw the strange bleached blonde from the day before sitting there.

Instead of looking scared or trying to shrink into the background, as a normal person would when a uniformed police officer was practically yelling at them in a public place, she smiled, stood, and sauntered—yes, sauntered—over to Ryan.

"Well, that's not a very nice way to greet a friend," she said. She actually reached out a hand and trailed her fingers down Ryan's uniform sleeve.

I looked at Sammy. Her normally pleasant demeanor had been replaced by what was very nearly a scowl. As near as Sammy could get to one, anyway.

Ryan pulled away from the woman. "We're not friends, Cheryl. And what did you do to your hair?"

She beamed and patted it. "Oh, you noticed? I thought you'd like it. I know how you feel about blondes." She looked directly at Sammy as she said it.

Sammy stepped closer to Ryan. Her blond ponytail swung with her movement. "Ryan?"

"Ignore her," Ryan said over his shoulder. He held an arm protectively back toward her. "She's leaving."

"I am?" Cheryl blinked innocently.

"Yes, you are," Ryan said firmly.

"You don't want to introduce us?" She pouted.

Before Ryan could say anything, I intervened. Whatever the woman's deal was, she was clearly trying to mess with Sammy, and I wasn't having it. "You've already met," I said, striding across the café toward her. I dropped Mike's coffee cup back on the counter—hopefully for good this time—as I approached her. "It's time for you to go." I put my hands on her shoulders and guided her toward the door.

"Ryan!" She twisted to try to get away from me,

but I kept moving her forward. "She's putting her hands on me, Ryan!"

Ryan ignored her.

"This is assault! She's assaulting me!"

I smiled at the book clubbers who were gawking at us as I hustled her by them.

"Ryan, arrest this woman! I want to press charges!"

"You can go down to the police station and swear out a warrant," Ryan said.

She stopped at the door, so I reached around her and pushed it open then nudged her shoulder until she walked through it. When the door closed behind her, she turned around and stared in. I crossed my arms over my chest and stared back for an uncomfortably long time. My confidence was starting to waver, when she finally walked away. I exhaled and dropped my arms. I would have leaned against the door, but I still had my wits about me enough to remember that it opened out. Instead, I just stood there for a few seconds, taking deep breaths until I calmed down.

When I turned around, the book clubbers were still staring. I smiled. "Is there anything I can get for you ladies? Refills? Some more cookies?" They'd made a dent in the mountain of cookies in the middle of the table but still had probably a couple dozen left. They shook their heads almost in unison, probably afraid I'd escort them out next. But they were all good, paying customers who didn't seem to have some sort of odd obsession with my café manager, so I was more than happy to let them stay.

I walked back over to Sammy and Ryan. I said nothing but raised my eyebrows at Ryan, assuming that he was smart enough to know that I was looking for an explanation. He wasn't.

"Who is she?" Sammy asked after it became clear that he wasn't going to volunteer it. If it had been me asking, it would have almost unavoidably come out sounding angry and biting. Sammy, though, in her Sammy way, somehow managed to make it sound gentle, innocent, and maybe a little wounded.

Despite that, Ryan still managed to look immensely uncomfortable. "My ex-girlfriend," he muttered.

I looked at Sammy. She appeared to be okay with his answer. I wasn't, though.

"If she's your ex, why is she here? And why was she here yesterday?"

"She was here yesterday?" Ryan looked from me to Sammy. We both nodded. "Oh geez." Ryan raked a hand through his dark hair.

"Well?" I wasn't sure if he was actually

distracted by the news that it was the second day in a row his ex had been in to Antonia's or if he was dodging the question, but either way, I wasn't going to let him get away with it.

"Cheryl has—" He paused and looked between the two of us. "She has boundary issues."

"Boundary issues?" I repeated. "What kind of boundary issues?"

Ryan shifted his weight uncomfortably from one foot to the other. "She just—she just has trouble believing that it's over," he stammered.

"And how long has it been over?" I asked. It probably wasn't any of my business, but I felt as if I had to stand up for Sammy. It wasn't in her temperament to do it for herself.

"Like ten years."

"Ten *years*?" I was sure I'd heard him wrong. Ten years ago, Ryan would have been in high school. Even Sammy looked shocked.

Ryan rubbed the back of his neck and nodded. "We broke up right after we graduated high school. I was going away to school and wanted to be able to date other people, and I guess somehow she thought I meant that I was coming back to her someday."

"Because that's what you told her?"

"No! I told her we were done. She just doesn't give up!"

I looked at Sammy. She looked as if she was deep in thought, possibly trying to decide if she believed him. I sure didn't.

"So what you're trying to tell us is that you broke up with her ten years ago and went away to college, and she just somehow magically knew that you live here now and are dating Sammy? And knew Sammy's *name*?" For the first time, neither of them reacted to me saying that the two of them were dating. Either they'd given up on pretending to hide it, or they were completely thrown off by Cheryl's visit.

"You have to believe me," Ryan said. "I haven't talked to her for years! I don't know how she finds this stuff out, but she does!"

"*She's done this before?*" I was really mad now, and it was clearly showing, because Sammy reached out and touched my arm.

"It's okay, Fran. She's gone. And after you escorting her out like that, I'm sure she won't be back."

I wished I had the confidence that she did, but I didn't. And from the look on his face, I didn't think Ryan did either.

Chapter 16

BY THE TIME Sammy poked her head into the back room later that afternoon to tell me that Mrs. Bayless and Mrs. Crawford—the school secretaries —were there looking for me, I had completely forgotten that they were coming, and I wasn't sure I was excited about it. Mike's revelation that there was video of the murder had pretty much doomed my investigation. And if it hadn't, his tirade about how I was messing with his case as well as a kid's life would have taken the wind out of its sails. But it would have been rude to back out when they were already there, and they didn't know I had invited them to try to get dirt on Veronica Underwood, so I decided to just go out there and have a nice cup of coffee and a chat about our holiday plans or some other innocuous topic.

My plan was clearly not their plan, however.

"So I assume you want to know more about Veronica," Mrs. Bayless said within seconds of us all sitting down.

I stared at her, completely dumbfounded. How had she known?

Mrs. Bayless chuckled and shared a glance with Mrs. Crawford. "We may be old, dear, but we're not dumb!"

"You can't let your mind get slow when you're dealing with teenagers all day!" Mrs. Crawford added.

"Oh, heavens no! They look for any chance to pull one over on you! Turning in notes 'from their parents'"—Mrs. Bayless made dramatic air quotes as she said it—"that are written in text speak."

"Claiming their teacher sent them to the office as a reward for good behavior," Mrs. Crawford said.

"Coming to us instead of the nurse because they're too ill to go to her office and they need to go home now."

"They always want to drive themselves home in that case. They're too sick to sit in a classroom, but they're completely fine to drive."

Mrs. Bayless nodded seriously, as if it were the truest statement she'd ever heard.

"Oh, Marian, do you remember the boy who tried to tell us we couldn't call his parents to pick him up when he got sent home for fighting because they were out of the country?"

"And then his father came walking down the hall? Of course!"

"Who was that?" Mrs. Crawford asked.

"You don't remember? It was Mike Stanton! That's why it was so remarkable! He was the straightest-laced boy we've probably ever had, so it was a shock that he was getting sent home, and then his father was the police chief coming in to give a career day talk that day!"

"Oh, that's right!" Mrs. Crawford laughed. "You know Mike Stanton, don't you, Franny? You're about the same age, aren't you?"

Mrs. Bayless interrupted before I could say anything, which was good because I was too busy being shocked by Mike getting in trouble back in high school. "Of course she knows Mike! They're friends! She's worked with him on all the murder cases!"

That snapped me out of my shock. "Whoa! I don't think you could call what I've done 'working *with* him.' I know he sure wouldn't call it that." I wasn't sure he would call me his friend anymore either, but I didn't think it was necessary to bring that up.

"You're the one who's solved all the murders, aren't you?" Mrs. Bayless asked indignantly.

"Well, I—I mean, I—" I tried to stammer out a protest, but Mrs. Crawford cut me off.

"Now, Marian, you know Franny's far too polite to take all the credit." Mrs. Crawford reached out and patted my hand then left hers there. "We know the truth, and that's all that matters. Besides, we're not here to talk about the murders she's already solved! We're here to talk about the one she still has to!"

"But it's already solved," I protested. Whether I thought they had the right person or not, Mike had scared me off of pursuing it any further.

"Oh, nonsense!" Mrs. Crawford said. "That murder's no more solved than we're retiring this year."

I looked from one of them to the other.

Mrs. Bayless patted my hand, so now I was practically holding hands with the two ladies. "What she means, dear, is that every year we say we're going to retire at the end of the year, but we never do, do we, Alice?"

"No, we don't, Marian!" Mrs. Crawford looked

at me meaningfully. "It's the kids that keep us coming back, you know."

I nodded as sympathetically as I could.

"Now, about Veronica's murder!" Mrs. Crawford thankfully let go of my hand as she reached for one of the cookies I'd placed in the middle of the table. "What theories do you have so far?"

"Theories? I don't really have any. And from what I understand, even if I did, it wouldn't matter, because the police have the murder on videotape."

The ladies looked at each other. I could tell this was news to them.

"They most certainly do not!" Mrs. Bayless said, to my surprise. She, too, released my hand and went for a cookie.

"They do. Mike told me," I said, folding my hands in front of me to discourage any future hand-holding.

"They don't! The camera that points to that part of the parking lot is broken, and it has been for weeks!"

"But Mike—"

"I don't know what Mike told you, but I look at those cameras every day, and the camera that points to that part of the parking lot is broken," Mrs. Crawford said.

"Maybe there was another camera somewhere?

Off school property somewhere?" It sounded weak even to me, but Mike said there was video evidence.

"I don't think so! Not with all the trees between the school and the road!"

"But it's December."

"They're pine trees!"

I realized she was right. But even if she was right and Mike, despite being in charge of the case, was somehow wrong, I still wasn't sure I wanted to pursue the investigation any further. I was still feeling stunned from Mike's visit.

The three of us sat there for several moments, the two of them munching away on their cookies and me simultaneously trying to reconcile the fact that there couldn't be video of the murder with Mike's assertion that there was, all while trying to fight my returning impulse to get back into the investigation.

"So now that that's sorted out, who are your suspects?" Mrs. Bayless asked.

"I don't have any," I said, still determined to not get myself any more involved.

"No need to be humble around us, dear. Just tell us what you think, and we'll tell you our opinion," Mrs. Bayless said.

"I—I really don't know," I said, though what I meant was that I really didn't want to talk about it.

The ladies looked at me and then at each other.

"Maybe she's run into a dead end and needs some help," Mrs. Crawford said to Mrs. Bayless, as though I weren't even there.

"Good point, Alice," Mrs. Bayless replied before turning back to me. "How about we tell you what we think, and you can go from there? Sound good? Good."

I hadn't had a chance to say anything, and it didn't look as if she was planning on giving me one.

"To start, it's obvious that Ann didn't kill her," Mrs. Bayless said.

"Obvious," Mrs. Crawford echoed.

"She's far too kind to even think about such a thing."

Mrs. Crawford nodded.

"The poor thing would have been justified in it if she had, what with all the abuse she put up with during that play."

"If you ask me, Marcus was cruel to have Ann as the co-director. Gwen would have at least been able to fight back!"

"Veronica wouldn't have made it as long as she did if Gwen had been her co-director."

Despite my decision not to talk about it, they'd piqued my curiosity. "Wait, Marcus—Marcus Varros? The principal?"

They nodded in unison.

"And Gwen is—"

"Gwen Blarney," Mrs. Bayless said. "She was the drama teacher before Veronica came. She and Ann directed the plays together, but Ann was really just there to assist. Gwen did most of the work. She was so upset when Marcus told her she wouldn't be involved anymore!"

"Well, of course she was. She worked for years to get the rights to the play!" Mrs. Crawford looked pointedly at me. "You have to get the rights, you know. You can't just go putting on any play you feel like!"

"Gwen had wanted to put on this play for years. They didn't want to let a high school put it on, but Gwen kept at it, and she finally got them to agree! She was so excited. I remember the day last year she came in to tell Marcus."

"And then over the summer, he tells us not just that she's not directing, but she's not even teaching the drama classes anymore!"

Mrs. Bayless shook her head mournfully. "It was completely out of the blue."

"She didn't know he was hiring a new drama teacher?" I asked.

They shook their heads.

"None of us did," Mrs. Bayless said.

"We were all very surprised. He just came in one day and said he had hired a new drama teacher and she would be directing the play with Ann."

"Gwen was devastated."

"And angry!"

"She was angry?" I asked.

They both nodded.

"She deserved to be!" Mrs. Crawford said.

I nodded. "It sounds like it." I looked down at my fingers before starting to speak cautiously. "You don't think—"

They looked at each other, seeming to silently communicate something or other. After as many years as they'd worked together, I didn't doubt they were capable of it.

Finally, Mrs. Bayless spoke. "You have to know that Gwen is really a lovely young woman."

"Lovely," Mrs. Crawford echoed.

"But with getting pushed out of her job and getting the play taken from her so suddenly by such an ill-tempered woman, well…" She trailed off with a shrug and glanced at Mrs. Crawford.

"You can see how she could be driven to murder," Mrs. Crawford finished for her.

I was briefly taken aback by her bluntness, but then I realized that they were telling me exactly what I had wanted to know—who other than Ann

Crowsdale might have had a motive to murder Veronica Underwood. And as much as I knew that, for the sake of whatever threads of friendship still existed between Mike and me, I should stay out of it, they were handing me a suspect and motive. If I left Brett alone and went about my investigation quietly and discreetly, maybe I could keep it up. At least, just enough to see if there was anything to this Gwen Blarney angle.

I nodded at the women. "That's interesting about Gwen. I hadn't heard all that before."

"So you'll look into it?" Mrs. Crawford asked.

"Not that we want to get Gwen in any trouble, but—" Mrs. Bayless turned her hands palms up, as if to say that they couldn't help it.

"But you want to help Ann Crowsdale," I finished for her.

They glanced at each other and nodded.

I took a deep breath. "While we're on the subject, was there anyone else on the staff who had particular trouble with Veronica Underwood?"

"*Particular* trouble?" Mrs. Bayless asked. "Well, no, not as far as I could say. They all had *some* trouble with her, but Gwen was really the one who had the worst of it."

"And Ann, of course," Mrs. Crawford said.

"But that's because she had to work so closely

with her on the play, you know," Mrs. Bayless clari-
fied, seemingly both to Mrs. Crawford and me.

"Of course, of course. Everyone else could
avoid her."

"So no one else on the staff." I paused and got
ready to watch their faces to gauge for their reaction. "What about any of the students?"

They looked at each other for a long moment
then back at me.

"Well, dear, is there anyone in particular you're
asking about?" Mrs. Bayless asked.

I decided to play dumb. "No, not in particular. I
was just thinking that the staff could avoid her, but
the students couldn't. Maybe she had some conflicts
with one of them."

They looked at each other again.

"Is there something you've heard?" Mrs. Bayless
asked.

I tried to look innocent and unsuspecting. I
shrugged. "Just that she and Brett Wallace got into
some kind of screaming match at the play practice
right before she died."

They exchanged another glance. I was starting
to wonder if there was something they knew. But if
they did, I had no idea whether it was something
they were trying to hide from me or waiting for me
to guess.

"That's true," Mrs. Bayless said.

I waited for a few seconds in hopes that she would volunteer more information, but she didn't. "Did any other students have trouble with her like that?"

Fortunately, they didn't look at each other this time, because I probably would have said something about it if they had. Mrs. Bayless just answered on her own. "No, and we would have heard about something like that if it had. Veronica wasn't shy about sending students to the office who disagreed with her, even if it was just about the color pen they were using."

"Seriously?" I asked. That seemed pretty crazy, even for someone as irascible as Veronica Underwood.

"Oh yes. That sweet Amanda who works for you got sent to the office for using a purple pen instead of black."

"On her own notes!" Mrs. Crawford added.

"The poor thing was in tears. I didn't even send her in to talk to Marcus. I just let her sit and calm herself down and then sent her on to her next class when the bell rang."

I tried to picture Amanda getting in trouble. I couldn't even begin to. The girl was a model employee and quiet as a church mouse—I'd never had to so much as remind her to smile when she took a customer's order. For her to get in trouble for something as minor as using the wrong color pen on her own notes, Veronica must have been even worse than I thought. But Brett was apparently the only kid who had ever yelled back. "So Brett is the only one who ever really got into a confrontation with her?"

The ladies both nodded.

"That boy has no fear," Mrs. Crawford said.

Well, that left only one thing to ask. "Do you think he could have…?" I trailed off and let them fill in the gap, which they readily did, demonstrating the fact with another look between them.

"Brett certainly puts effort into projecting a very —" Mrs. Bayless paused "—shall we say, *aggressive* persona."

"Projecting?"

Mrs. Bayless gave me a look that I assumed was supposed to communicate something, but I wasn't sure what. All she said was, "Brett is a complex young man."

I looked at Mrs. Crawford, who seemed to be the more blunt of the two, but she was studying her coffee. I decided to leave the question of Brett at that. I picked up one of the gingerbread men and bit his head off.

"Marian, do you think—" Mrs. Crawford started, looking up from her coffee at Mrs. Bayless. "The young lady—" They looked at each other for several seconds before Mrs. Bayless turned to me.

"Veronica did have a young lady come looking for her the day before she died," Mrs. Bayless said.

"She did? Who was it?" I asked.

"I can't recall her name at the moment, but I can look it up in the visitor log for you tomorrow."

"That would be great, thank you. Do you know what the woman wanted?"

They did their meaningful-look thing again before Mrs. Bayless answered. "She said she was a friend of Veronica's, but she didn't seem very friendly."

"She seemed angry," Mrs. Crawford interjected.

I wondered why it had taken so long for them to bring this up. They'd readily thrown Gwen Blarney's name out there, but I had been about to excuse myself when they mentioned this new woman. Either they really didn't like Gwen, or they really suspected her of killing Veronica Underwood. Whichever it was, I was interested in finding out more about Veronica's visitor. "Do you know what she was angry about?"

"No, but she was even more upset when Veronica refused to see her," Mrs. Bayless said.

"What did she do?"

"She left."

"She left?" I had been expecting something much more dramatic. An angry friend of Veronica's should have thrown a temper tantrum, yelled, broken some things. Compared to what I was expecting, leaving was kind of disappointing.

"Stormed out," Mrs. Crawford said.

"Do you know if she ever found Veronica?"

Mrs. Crawford raised her eyebrows at me with a pointed look. "That's a very good question."

I looked at Mrs. Bayless. She didn't seem to disagree, but it still seemed odd that she hadn't thought to volunteer the information about Veronica's visitor until Mrs. Crawford prompted her. Had it just slipped her mind? She was getting up there in years, after all. A memory lapse here and there was to be expected. Or was she really that sure Gwen Blarney was involved?

And then another possibility entered my mind. Gwen Blarney could just be a convenient scapegoat to get the much-beloved Ann Crowsdale off the hook. Or worse, perhaps she was being set up to go down for the crime as a result of some personal grudge Mrs. Bayless had against her. She didn't seem like the type to scheme to put an innocent woman in jail, but maybe I was letting her grandmotherly looks and persona cloud my vision. I had a lot to think about. But first—"Is there anything else either of you can think of?"

They shook their heads in unison.

"And you'll find the woman's name for me?" I asked Mrs. Bayless.

"First thing tomorrow," she replied.

I nodded and got ready to excuse myself, but Mrs. Bayless stopped me before I could stand.

"Don't go yet! We've talked all about that awful Veronica but not at all about you! We want to know all about how you've been since you graduated! You're seeing that nice Matt Cardosi, aren't you?"

"I am."

"Well, we want to hear all about it!"

I sat with them for nearly another hour, answering all their questions about my life from the time I went away to college up through my recent trip to Italy with Matt. By the time they declared that it was time to go to their homes to fix dinner for their husbands, I was all talked out for, by my best guess, the next week or so. But I did have one more thing I knew I needed to talk to someone about—or ask them, anyway.

I managed to catch Sammy just before she went out the door. "Could you do me a favor? It's a pretty big one."

"You want me to open *and* close the café tomorrow?" she asked with a grin.

"I wish it were that easy," I said.

Her gaze grew suspicious. "What do you need me to do?"

"Mike told me there's video evidence of Ann Crowsdale murdering Veronica Underwood. But Mrs. Bayless said the school's camera that points that way is broken." I took a deep breath. "I need you to find out from Ryan exactly what the police have and what it shows."

Sammy stared at me for an uncomfortably long moment. I was asking her to take advantage of her mostly unacknowledged relationship with Ryan to get inside information on a police investigation. But it was an investigation she herself had asked me to get involved with.

After a long enough pause that I'd begun to assume the answer was no, she nodded. "I'll do it. Whatever I have to do to help Ann."

I could only hope it would help Ann. The other possibility was that it would prove to all of us—beyond a shadow of a doubt—that she was guilty.

Chapter 17

FIRST THING THE NEXT MORNING, I headed to Cape Bay High for my meeting with Principal Marcus Varros. Walking down the hall past the already-full classrooms, I felt the same ridiculous missing-hall-pass anxiety as I had the week before when I'd gone to the school to see Veronica Underwood. I wondered how many visits it would take to get over it. Not that I particularly planned to be visiting the high school on a regular basis. Especially not on murder-related business.

"Good morning, Franny!" Mrs. Bayless chirped as I opened the office door.

"Good morning, Mrs. Bayless!"

"Good morning, Franny!" Mrs. Crawford's voice came from somewhere in the back.

"Good morning!" I called back.

"I'll just let Marcus know you're here, and then you can go back," Mrs. Bayless said. She stood up from her desk and went back to the open door behind her. "Franny Amaro is here for you, Marcus."

I cringed just a little at her calling me Franny. Not that I minded her calling me that—I just hoped the principal didn't think that was the name I usually went by.

It was.

"Franny, come in!" the man boomed from somewhere I couldn't see.

I sighed then plastered on a big smile and headed for his office.

As I passed Mrs. Bayless, she shoved a piece of paper in my hand. "The information you asked for," she said.

I nodded. Veronica's angry visitor. "Thank you."

I stepped into Varros's office, and Mrs. Bayless closed the door behind me.

"Good to meet you, Franny. Marcus Varros." Varros stood up from behind his desk and stuck out his hand for me to shake. "Have a seat."

I sat down in one of the chairs across the desk from him and immediately felt tiny in comparison to him. Was the chair lower than a normal chair? Was his extra tall? Were my two-decade-old anxieties about being sent to the principal's office messing with my head and making me imagine that he was looming over me when he wasn't?

"So what can I do for you today, Franny?" he asked.

"Uh, Fran," I said. "You can call me Fran."

He chuckled good-naturedly. "Fran it is. Now what can I do for you?"

I gave him the same line I'd given Mrs. Bayless about needing some forms filled out for my taxes since I was donating the refreshments for the play.

"Not a problem," he said, and I handed him the basic, vaguely official-looking documents I'd cobbled together the night before. "I can go ahead and fill these out for you if you don't mind waiting here a few minutes."

"That would be perfect!" I said. And it would be. It would give me time to try to engage him in conversation about Veronica Underwood's murder. I waited for several seconds while he got started filling out the first form in hopes that he'd be focused enough on that to not pay too much attention to what I was talking about. "I was sorry to hear about Veronica's murder," I finally said. "It must be quite a loss to the school community."

"Mm, terribly unfortunate," he mumbled.

"She was a new hire this year, right?"

"Mm-hmm."

This wasn't going well. "When I made my appointment, Mrs. Bayless said that the play was being taken over by a, uh—" I pretended Gwen Blarney's name wasn't on the tip of my tongue. "What was her name again?"

"Gwen. Gwen Blarney."

"That's right! Is she new to the school also?"

"No, Gwen's been here." He wasn't even looking up.

"Oh, well, that should make it easier on her. What does she teach?"

"English."

His simple answers were starting to frustrate me, but maybe he was just that focused on the paperwork. Or maybe I was asking the wrong questions. "That's a big job, stepping into a play right before it opens like that. Do you think she's going to do okay?"

"She was our play director before Veronica."

"Oh really? Was she looking for a change?"

He looked up at me slowly. "What exactly are you trying to get at, Fran?"

I looked up at him from my maybe-too-low chair and smiled. "Just making conversation."

He put his pen down. "It seems like you're doing more than trying to make conversation."

"Oh, I, um—" I stalled to think of something that wasn't quite the truth. I figured it wouldn't go so well to tell him I was trying to get the charges dropped against one of his teachers at the expense of putting another in jail. Of course, there was also that woman who had come to visit Veronica. The secretaries hadn't said that he knew anything about her, but maybe they'd just failed to mention it—as they'd nearly failed to mention her visit at all. But still, I didn't feel that it would do to show my hand too soon. "I'm just curious, I guess," I said with a shrug.

His eyes narrowed. "You're one of the people who thinks Ann couldn't possibly have done it, aren't you?"

I tried to seem uninterested. "I've only met her once. She seemed nice, but what do I know?" I waited a few seconds while he appraised me. "What do you think? I mean, you must not be too thrilled about losing two of your teachers in one go. And both of the play directors, right?"

Varros nodded then leaned back in his large leather chair, making it rock. It had to be on the maximum height. I'd seen the man standing up just a few minutes before, and he hadn't been a giant.

There was no way he was that tall. He tented his fingers and drummed them against each other. "Yes, they were our two directors." He shook his head. "One dead and the other arrested for her murder. It's hard to believe."

I waited to see if he'd say anything else. He didn't, so figuring I had nothing to lose, I decided to push the question. "Do you believe it?"

He sighed heavily and put his hands on the back of his head. "I don't know what I believe. The police certainly believe it was Ann, don't they?"

"They seem to."

"But it doesn't seem like anyone else in the town does, do they?"

"No, they don't."

He rocked forward again and folded his hands on his desk. "You know, I've racked my brain, ever since it happened, trying to picture Ann killing someone, and I have to admit, I can't imagine it. She's such a good, kind person, you know?"

I nodded as though I had a longer history with her than I did.

"But the police wouldn't have arrested her if they didn't have evidence, so..." He turned his palms up and shrugged.

I couldn't let him skirt the issue. "But what if they made a mistake? I hate to think about it, but it's possible. You seem to have known Veronica better than maybe most of the people in town—"

Before I could finish my sentence, he cut me off.

"What do you mean by that?" he asked sharply.

I instinctively pulled away from him. "Just that —I mean, you hired her—"

Varros relaxed back in his chair. He chuckled. "Oh, that. Whew! For a second there, I thought you were accusing *me* of murder."

I laughed along with him, good-naturedly, to keep him on my side. It was a PR trick I'd been taught my first week on the job—mirror the client to make them feel connected to you. "Oh no, no, no, not at all! I just thought you'd have more insight than someone who didn't know her as well."

"Of course, of course." He stared into the distance over my head. "Who else might have killed Veronica?" He tented his fingers and drummed them again. I wondered if it was something he did —along with the extra-high chair—to seem impos- ing. "You know, as I understand it, there was a young lady here the other day looking for her. From what Marian told me, she was very upset even before Veronica refused to see her."

I played dumb. "Do you know who she was? Or what she wanted?"

"Her name was Kristin. Kristin Mansmith. I'm not sure what she wanted, though."

I looked down discreetly at the paper Mrs. Bayless had passed me on my way in. It was a photocopy of a Rhode Island driver's license, and sure enough, the name on it was Kristin Mansmith. "You said she was upset—do you think she was upset enough to kill Veronica?"

"Well, I didn't speak with her, so I don't know. But she was very upset when Veronica wouldn't see her. She threatened to wait outside, but Marian told her she wouldn't be able to do that, and we'd have to call the police if she did. Not that we like doing that, of course, but it's a safety issue. We can't have people not associated with the school just hanging around the parking lot."

"Of course not."

He leaned in toward me across the desk. "Can I tell you something in confidence?"

I nodded, wondering what it could be that was supposed to be a secret but that he was comfortable telling a virtual stranger.

"It's in confidence because I don't think the police have released this piece of information, but I think it's relevant."

I nodded again. "My lips are sealed."

"Veronica's tires were slashed. All four of them.

The police said they thought the murderer did it to give themselves an opportunity. Stall her by her car long enough to attack her. Or 'talk' to her, if they couldn't manage that any other way." He made air quotes around the word "talk."

My stomach flip-flopped. It was so cold-blooded to set her up like that. Knowing that detail made me even more skeptical that Ann Crowsdale had done it. It was one thing for a normally kind-hearted woman to snap and kill her nasty coworker; it was entirely another for her to plot and carry out a murder. That would have taken an amount of ice in her veins that I found it difficult to imagine she'd managed to hide from everyone in town.

"So you think this Kristin Mansmith could have slashed Veronica's tires to keep her in the parking lot so she could kill her?"

"I imagine she may not have meant to kill her. Maybe she really wanted to just talk. But something went wrong, and she lost her temper and killed her."

"Did you tell the police this theory?"

"I did. But apparently they found poor Ann to be a more convincing suspect."

I remembered the issue of the video evidence Mike had mentioned. I hadn't had a chance to talk to Sammy yet that morning to see what, if anything, she'd found out from Ryan about the video, but sitting there with Varros—who seemed to have some inside information—was a good opportunity to fish for more information. "You don't have any video cameras on the parking lot?" I asked.

"We do," Varros said. "But one of them has been broken for a few weeks now, and unfortunately, it's the one that covered the area where Veronica parked."

"So it didn't get the murder or whoever slashed her tires," I said. "That's a shame."

"It is, it is."

I thought of something. "Who knew that the camera was broken?"

"Everyone who worked in the school," he said, dashing my hopes of that being a piece of information only Varros and the secretaries had. "We discussed it at the last staff meeting."

"What about the students?" I asked.

"Some of them would have known. We have several of them who help out in the office during the day. It's likely they could have overheard us discussing it." His eyebrows knit together. "Why do you ask about students?"

I shrugged nonchalantly. "Just curious."

"Are you suggesting a student could have been involved in Veronica's murder?" I didn't know whether he sounded more incredulous or indignant, but it was one of those I words.

"I heard she might have had conflicts with some of the students. Like Brett Wallace."

"You think Brett was involved?"

"I'm just saying I heard they got in a screaming match the day she died. He's a… troubled boy, isn't he?"

"Whatever Brett's problems are, he's not a murderer. Now, is there anything else? I have another meeting in a few minutes."

"My tax papers," I said, feeling like I'd hit a nerve mentioning Brett.

He glanced at the papers. From where I was sitting, I could tell he'd only gotten partway through the first one, and there were three. Varros finishing the paperwork would give me some more time to fish for information.

But I had no such luck.

"I'll finish these and give them back to you when you bring the food to the play." He stood up and extended his hand. "It was nice to meet you, Fran."

I stood too and shook his hand, knowing when I was being dismissed. "You too, Marcus." I knew when to cut my losses, but I also knew when I had to take advantage of diminishing opportunities. As I reached the door, I turned back around. Varros was walking around his desk, presumably to make sure I went ahead and got out. "What about Gwen Blarney?" I asked. "Do you think she could have killed Veronica to get the play back?"

He looked at me coolly. I had clearly worn out my welcome. "She could have. Gwen is a very ambitious woman, and she was not pleased when I moved her to the English department. Now, if you'll excuse me, I have other things to attend to."

I opened the door and saw Brett Wallace sitting in the chairs outside Varros's office.

"Hey, Fran!" he said, cracking a smile when he saw me.

"Hi, Brett."

"I didn't know nosy baristas could get sent to the principal's office."

I bit my tongue to keep from making a snarky comment in return that would have been inappropriate for an adult to make to a boy who was little more than a child.

"I assume you're here to see me, Mr. Wallace?" Varros asked from behind me. I glanced back over my shoulder and noticed that he was, in fact, normal height and not some giant like the chairs in his office made him seem.

Brett got up and shoved his hands deep in the

pockets of his low-slung pants. "Yeah, teachers are touchy about getting flipped off."

I heard Varros sigh. "Come on in."

Brett winked as he walked past me. I ignored him.

I said my goodbyes to Mrs. Bayless and Mrs. Crawford, promising them we'd have coffee again soon. It took a good fifteen minutes to extract myself, but I was finally out in the hallway, heading out to my car. I didn't usually drive much of anywhere in Cape Bay because it was so small, but the school was on the edge of town, and I'd been running late after taking a few extra minutes to play with Latte that morning.

A teacher came through a door and started walking down the hall toward me. I had that same surge of nervousness and, for just a second, looked for a door I could jump into to avoid getting caught in the hall. But then I remembered that I was an adult and tried to relax a little.

As the teacher and I moved past each other, I thought she might have been Gwen Blarney, from the way the secretaries had described her to me.

"I was sorry to hear about Veronica," I blurted even though she was behind me.

Her footsteps stopped, and she turned around, her eyebrows raised. "Veronica was not a very nice woman," she said. "But thank you for your condolences." She turned back around and continued on her way.

Apparently Gwen Blarney had no qualms about speaking ill of the dead. And if she was that comfortable being critical of Veronica while she was dead, how much must she have hated her in life? As I walked out of the school, I was pretty sure Gwen had moved ahead of Brett on my suspect list. Now I just had to track down Kristin Mansmith to see where she fit into it all.

Chapter 18

IN ADDITION to the photocopy of Kristin Mansmith's driver's license—a part of the school's security protocol—the paper Mrs. Bayless gave me had a phone number scribbled on it and a note: "Staying at the Surfside."

The Surfside Inn was Cape Bay's biggest and best hotel, which was to say that it was Cape Bay's *only* real hotel. Or motel, as the case may be. It wasn't the only place people could stay in our little beach town, of course, but all the rest were either bed-and-breakfasts or rental houses. The houses were where families tended to stay, the bed-and-breakfasts where couples stayed, and the Surfside was where, well, everyone else stayed.

I got in my car and drove over, still feeling weird

about driving around Cape Bay but not wanting to divert all the way back to my house to drop the car off and then walk back across town to the Surfside. Besides, it was cold outside, and my car was warm.

The Surfside Inn wasn't a bad little place, but it had seen better days. The exterior that I remembered having been blue and white in my childhood was now bluish gray and gray. I'd seen the inside of one of the rooms fairly recently, and while it wasn't the newest, it seemed to be kept fairly clean. The pool, drained for the winter, looked sad with its cracked tiles and puddle of murky green rainwater in the deep end. It was only the beginning of the season, though, and with our brutal winters, people tended to save their repairs up until the weather calmed down in the spring. I hoped that was what the owners of the Surfside were doing and not just letting the place fall apart.

I went into the motel's office. I noted with pleasure that the teenager who had been supposedly working the reception desk—but was actually completely absorbed in his phone—the last time I'd been in was missing. I knew the little twerp was probably a seasonal employee and, even if he wasn't, was probably in school, but I preferred to think that his ineptitude and gross lack of customer service skills were the reason he wasn't there. No one else was at the desk either, but the door to the owner's office was open.

"Ed?" I called.

"C'mon in!" a voice called back.

I went back into the office and found Ed Martin sitting at his desk, peering at his computer. His wire-framed glasses were perched at the tip of his nose.

"Fran! Hi! How are ya?" he asked. "Have a seat. What can I do for you?"

"I'm looking for someone I think may be a guest here." I sat down in the chair across from him and noticed immediately that Ed seemed to be at a normal, appropriate height compared to me.

"This one's not dead, is he?" Ed asked.

"No. Well, I hope not." A murderer, maybe, but not a victim. The last time I'd been to the Surfside to ask Ed about one of his guests, the man had been a murder victim. Of course, if Kristin Mansmith was dead too, that would probably throw a wrench into the police's case against Ann Crowsdale. Unless she somehow managed to have a secret grudge against a woman from out of state too. "Her name's Kristin Mansmith." I realized it was probably a long shot that Kristin would still be there. It had been nearly a week since she'd gone into the school, looking for Veronica. Still, maybe I'd get lucky and she'd be in town for an extended visit.

"You're in luck!" Ed said. "Unless she died in the past hour or so, this one's still alive. I spoke to her just a little while ago when she called in to request a late checkout."

"She's still here? In Cape Bay?"

"For another hour or two."

"Which room?"

"Room 205."

"Thanks, Ed," I said, standing up from my normal-height chair. "Next time you come into Antonia's, your coffee's on me."

"Well then, I'll see you this afternoon!"

I laughed. "Sounds good. And thanks again!"

I left his office and climbed the outdoor stairs up to the second floor. I found room 205 but paused before raising my hand to knock. Varros thought this woman might have murdered Veronica Underwood, and here I was, about to knock on her motel room door and try to talk to her about it. It was stupid. The smart thing to do would be to walk away and forget that I ever thought about getting involved. Before common sense could prevail and put me off the investigation, I knocked. As soon as I did, there was a thud inside the room, followed by some enthusiastic swearing.

I froze, not sure what the noise had been and not sure if I should knock again or call through the door to see if the woman I'd heard creatively cursing was okay or just slink away and find another way to run into her, maybe in the motel office when she came to check out.

Before I could make up my mind, the door jerked open. The woman standing there was hunched over at the waist, holding her right foot in her left hand. "What do you want? I told the man I was checking out late." The woman practically spat the words at me. In fact, it was all I could do to keep from wiping my face. I also noticed that she said she *told* Ed she was checking out late, whereas Ed had said that she *requested* a late checkout. Granted, I'd only known this woman for about five seconds, but I had a feeling her account of the conversation was the more accurate one.

"Well?" she asked, apparently finding my split-second hesitation too long. She looked every bit as annoyed and disgusted with me as she sounded.

"Kristin? Kristin Mansmith?"

Her expression instantly darkened, and I felt a pang of fear. She dropped her foot and stood up mostly straight. "Who's asking?" Her hand gripped the motel room door, and I expected her to slam it in my face at any second.

Against my better judgment, I didn't turn and run. "I'm Fran. Fran Amaro."

"Do I know you, Fran Amaro?"

I briefly considered making up some kind of lie to tell her, but I got the feeling she was experienced in that department and nothing I could come up with while standing there would convince her. I found myself wishing I had a few good lies pre-prepared, but I didn't, so I told the truth. "Nope."

"Then why are you here?"

Now I really wished I had a good lie in my back pocket. But none had materialized, so I went with the truth again. "Because I heard you were at the high school, looking for Veronica Underwood, the day before she died."

"Are you with the cops? I already talked to the cops." She started to close the door. I put my hand out to stop it.

"I'm not a cop."

"A reporter then. I don't talk to reporters." She tried to close the door again.

"I'm not a reporter."

"Then why do you care if I was looking for Ronnie?"

I took a deep breath. As much as I didn't like it, I was committed to the truth, no matter how scary it was. "I think the police may have arrested the wrong person for her murder, and I'm trying to figure out who else might have done it."

She stared at me for a long, uncomfortable moment during which I completely expected her to slam the door in my face or maybe pull out a gun and shoot me dead right there. But instead, she laughed. "Seriously?"

"Yes, seriously."

She laughed again then, to my surprise, pushed the door further open. "Come on in then. I only have a few minutes, but you can talk to me while I pack."

After a split second's hesitation—I did think this woman might be a murderer, after all—I followed her as she limped back into the motel room, favoring the right foot she'd been holding when she opened the door.

The room was much like the other one I'd been in—definitely not the newest or fanciest but fairly clean and well maintained. Except, of course, for the mountain of pizza boxes and fast food wrappers and bags on the dresser, but I assumed that hadn't been there before she checked in.

"Is your foot okay?" I asked, glancing around the room for anything that looked like a deadly weapon. There was nothing obvious, unless she was going to bash my head in with a lamp.

"Yeah, it's fine," she muttered. "Just dropped my laptop on it."

I winced in sympathy. That must have been the thud I'd heard when I knocked. "Is your laptop okay?"

"Yeah," she said and slung what I assumed was the offending device into the suitcase that lay open on the bed. I was close enough to see the Cape Bay High School sticker on it that I assumed meant it was not actually Kristin's laptop, but I kept my mouth shut. "So why do you care who killed Ronnie? You weren't a friend of hers."

I saw an opportunity for a stretching of the truth. If Kristin lived in Providence, there was no way she knew everyone "Ronnie" hung out with in Cape Bay. "How do you know? You don't live here," I replied, evoking my best tough girl, as I had with Brett.

Kristin just laughed. "Because you're too straightlaced. Ronnie would never hang out with someone like you."

"What? What do you mean?" I asked. I mean, I couldn't really argue with the fact that I had a tendency to be pretty straightlaced, but I didn't think there was any way for her to know that, especially not three minutes after meeting me.

"Are you kidding? Look at you!"

I glanced down at my black pea coat, blue sweater, and jeans. There was nothing I could see that was remarkable about them. I looked back at her blankly.

"You're just so"—she made some vague gesture at me with both hands—"so neat. So put together. And let me guess—you have a nice job, something cute and small town that gives you lots of time to wander around town, doing whatever you want. A bakery maybe?"

Apparently I was right in my initial assessment that no quickly assembled lie would trick her. I resigned myself to the truth. "A coffee shop."

She laughed. "Even better! And you probably have a great relationship with your parents, who have been married for forty years, and a nice boyfriend who supports you."

"My mother is dead, and my father skipped out on us when I was little," I said coldly.

She shrugged. "But I'm right about the boyfriend, aren't I?"

"Yeah." It was the first and only time I'd ever wished Matt weren't the really great boyfriend that he was.

"Yeah, see, Ronnie would never hang out with you."

"Because I have a boyfriend?"

"No, because at night you go home and cuddle on the couch with your boyfriend and crochet or something instead of going out and partying."

She had me there. "You're right. We weren't friends. I only met her once, and it was when I went to talk to her about a bake sale during the school play."

Kristin laughed again and clapped her hands. "It's even better than I thought."

I sighed. "But just because I wasn't her friend doesn't mean I want to see her killer go free."

"You don't trust the police? I figured a Goody Two-Shoes like you couldn't possibly imagine the police getting anything wrong."

"The woman they arrested is even more of a Goody Two-Shoes than I am. I don't think she killed Veronica, and neither does anyone else in town. Except the police, of course."

Kristin looked me up and down. "So you're going to solve it on your own?"

I shrugged. "I'm going to try."

She turned back to her suitcase and started throwing things in on top of the computer that wasn't hers. "So what do you want from me?"

"First of all, I want to know why you were looking for Veronica."

"We were roommates back in Providence. She left me on the hook for the whole lease when she moved here and skipped out on the last month's rent, so I came to get my money from her."

"And did you?"

"Indirectly."

I took a deep breath and glanced behind me. The door was still open. If Kristin made a move to come after me, I could run. I wasn't sure if I could get away, but I could run. Ignoring the little voice in my head telling me to shut up, I asked the question I knew I had to. "By killing her?"

Kristin turned to me slowly. I couldn't read the look on her face, but it scared me, maybe even more so because I couldn't read it. "What did you say?"

I took a step back. As far as I could see, her hands were empty, but that didn't mean she couldn't come after me with her fists and finger-nails. I didn't want that to happen. I liked having eyes. But I couldn't back down now. "I asked if your way of indirectly getting your money back from her was to kill her." I swallowed hard. Every muscle in my body was as tense as it had ever been as I got ready to turn and run.

But instead she laughed again. It was a habit of hers that kept me decidedly off balance. "You think I killed Ronnie over rent money?"

I wasn't sure which part she was objecting to—the killing or the rent money. I tried to look confident. "You were angry when she wouldn't see you. Maybe you didn't mean to do it, but she refused to pay, and in a fit of rage, you killed her."

She laughed harder. "Over rent money?"

"Stranger things have happened."

"You think I'd risk life in prison over a couple thousand bucks in rent money?"

I shrugged nonchalantly, but my confidence was waning.

"Hell no! I got her computer and called it even."

"So you didn't slash her tires to keep her at the school so you could talk to her?"

It was as if it were the funniest thing she'd ever heard. "Where did you get that idea?"

"Um, the principal at the school?" I suggested hesitantly. I tried to think back to whether he'd said it explicitly or whether it was just something I'd inferred from the other things he'd said, but it was hard with Kristin laughing in my face.

"Varros? Varros told you that?" She laughed harder. "He would." She threw the last of her things in the suitcase and zipped it closed. "No, I didn't kill Ronnie. I was still trying to get a hold of her when I heard she'd gotten her head smashed in."

"So how did you get her computer?"

She looked at me as if I was stupid. "You really are a goody-goody. I picked the lock at her apartment and took it. It's not like she was going to use it anymore."

I thought the school might be able to find some continued use for what was, in fact, *their* laptop, but I didn't think Kristin was the type who would particularly care about a technicality like that. Her story made sense, though. She didn't seem overly concerned about my insinuation that she had actually killed her friend, so either she was a good actress—possible—or she really didn't do it. One thing still bothered me, though. "If Veronica's dead, and you have the computer, why are you still in town? Weren't you afraid the police would come looking for it?"

Again, the laugh. "No! And even if they did, it's not like they'd know that I stole it. I would have told them she gave it to me and would have broken back in to take something else." She paused thoughtfully. "She did have a really nice pair of diamond earrings my ex-boyfriend gave her."

"Wait, what?"

"They hooked up after I broke up with him for cheating on me." She shook her head. "They deserved each other."

It was my turn to shake my head. I couldn't even begin to understand this girl.

"Anyway," she said, picking up her suitcase, "I wasn't worried about the cops. Besides, it's a cute little town you got here. Nice little shops downtown and all. Hey! Is that coffee shop yours? With the little pictures on the coffee? Anthony's or whatever?"

"Antonia's. And yes, that's mine."

"Cool. It's a nice place. I'm going to stop by there on my way home to get some cookies and a giant cup of coffee to keep me awake. Are you headed back there? I can give you a ride."

"Um, no, thanks. I have my car. But thank you," I said babbling, baffled from her friendly turn. I wondered if I could have saved myself a lot of trouble by identifying myself as the woman who owned the coffee shop "with the little pictures on the coffee" up front or if she was just being nice now because she'd decided we were done talking.

She walked past me toward the door. "Good luck finding who killed Ronnie. But hey, be careful. Good girl like you isn't used to dealing with people like this. You're getting into some dangerous stuff."

She was almost at the door before I processed what she said. "Wait, what do you mean? People like what?"

"There's stuff you obviously don't know about. Good girl like you could get hurt," she said and disappeared out the door.

I ran after her. "How? By whom? People like what? Murderers?"

A young couple walking down by the pool looked up at me and then hurried away.

Kristin laughed. "Just be careful. You seem like a nice lady, even if you are a goody-goody."

I watched, dumbfounded, as she headed down the stairs. The thing was, she didn't know I'd been around more than my share of murderers in the past few months. At least, I hoped that was why she said it.

Chapter 19

"YOU'RE EARLY!" Sammy said as I walked into the café a little while later. I'd gone home to drop my car off and take Latte for a walk before heading into the café. It was mostly because I needed to do those things anyway, but also because I knew Kristin was headed to the café on her way out of town. It wasn't that I wanted to avoid her, but I knew I wasn't going to get anything else out of her, and seeing her would just make me want to try. I didn't want to risk making a scene, as I nearly had at the Surfside when I started yelling about murderers as that couple was walking by.

It was the late-morning lull by the time I got there, and there were only a few customers scattered around the café. Business would pick up again in about half an hour for the lunchtime rush, but at the moment, things were quiet. I was glad because it would give me the chance to see what—if anything—Sammy had managed to find out from Ryan. He had a tendency to be a talker, so I was optimistic.

"I had some things to take care of this morning." I dropped my jacket and purse off in the back, grabbed my apron, and came back out front.

"Murder investigation stuff?"

I nodded as I started to fix myself a double espresso. I needed the pick-me-up after what felt like a very long morning.

"Did you find anything out?"

I watched the espresso shots as they finished pouring into the cup, admiring the rich color. The crema was the perfect shade of brown and looked deliciously creamy. I took the first sip, letting the liquid swirl across my tongue. It was the perfect temperature—just a degree hotter would have been too hot to drink.

"I found some things out," I said. "But I'm not really sure what they mean yet." I took my second sip. Still delicious. "What about you? Did you get the chance to talk to Ryan?"

"Yup." She sighed and leaned against the counter.

"And?"

"They have video, but it's not of the actual murder. Apparently the camera that should cover that part of the parking lot is broken."

So the story was consistent. I nodded.

"Apparently Mike was pretty mad about that, especially when he found out it had been broken for a couple weeks. Ryan said the principal got quite a lecture from him about it."

As a recent recipient of one of Mike's so-called "lectures," I sympathized. I downed the rest of the espresso—I was an adherent of the three sips rule—and contemplated another. It would be a lot of caffeine, but…

"The footage they do have, I guess, is the problem. It shows Mrs. Crowsdale—I mean Ann—and Veronica walking to the parking lot together, then Ann walks to her car and goes back toward Veronica's with a tire iron. She's there for another couple of minutes and then walks away empty handed. Ryan said that all four of Veronica's tires had been slashed. I guess Ann told the police that she got the tire iron because Veronica wanted to get a head start on taking them off while she waited for Triple A, but Veronica didn't have one. He said Ann swore that, when she left, Veronica was alone and working on taking off the first tire."

"She just left her there alone in the cold to wait for Triple A?"

"I asked the same thing. Apparently Veronica told her to leave. Triple A was supposed to be there within fifteen minutes. They were, but she was already dead when they found her."

I started another double espresso. Despite the heat of the last one, I had gotten a chill.

We stood there and watched the espresso pour into the cup. Without even seeing the video, based on its description, I understood why the police found it persuasive. I picked up the cup and took a second to admire the crema. It was all I could see because I'd used a porcelain espresso cup, though I knew the body and the heart of the espresso lay beneath it, as perfect as the crema. I knew because I'd pulled hundreds of thousands, maybe millions of espresso shots in my life, and when the part I could see—the crema—was perfect, the body and heart were too. I remembered not understanding that when I was a child until my grandfather had explained to me how in coffee, like in life, what you could see could often tell you about what you couldn't see as well. Just like how Mike could guess what would have been in the video that didn't exist based on what he could see in the video that did. Unless…

"Did Ryan say whether there was any way to get to Veronica's car that wouldn't have been caught by one of the other cameras?" I asked.

"He didn't mention it. Why—" She caught herself. "You think someone else could have been there. Someone who wasn't caught by the camera."

I nodded.

"They would have had to be incredibly lucky or know that the camera was broken to avoid it, though."

"The whole staff knew. Varros said they talked about it in their staff meeting."

"So the murderer could be anyone."

It should have been a frightening thought, but Sammy and I grinned at each other. Despite the video evidence, it could be possible that someone other than Ann Crowsdale had killed Veronica Underwood. But we had to find out if our theory was plausible—if someone really could have gotten to Veronica's car without being caught by any of the cameras.

"Could you call Ryan to ask him if it's possible?" I asked just as the bell over the café's door jingled to announce the start of the lunchtime rush. It was a few minutes earlier than I expected it, but it wasn't as though there was really a specific time for it—it was just whenever people started coming in.

"I don't think I have to," Sammy said. She grinned and pointed over my shoulder.

I turned around. It wasn't the lunchtime rush—it was Ryan.

"Just the man we wanted to see!" I said.

"Well, that's the kind of welcome a guy likes!" he said. "You have some new cookies you need me to taste test or something?"

"No, but we have some gingerbread ones you can have."

He shrugged. "That's good too."

I handed one across the counter to him.

"So what's up?" He looked over at Sammy and winked. She blushed furiously. Ryan grinned.

"We have a question about the video evidence in Veronica Underwood's murder," I said.

Ryan's smile faded. "You know I can't talk about that."

I started to protest that he'd already talked to Sammy about it, but then I caught the look in his eye. He couldn't talk about it publicly. Or officially. Quietly with Sammy, yes. Openly in the café, no. Especially not when he was in uniform and on duty.

"Of course. I understand." I waited a couple seconds while he chewed on his gingerbread man's leg. "What about if I had a hypothetical question?"

He raised an eyebrow.

"About the café's cameras, of course."

He nodded.

"Well, I have a few, and they cover the whole café."

He nodded again. I was pretty sure he was playing along with what I was trying to do.

"Well, what if one of them was broken? So a part of the café wasn't covered?"

"Just one?"

"Just one. The other cameras would pick up enough so that you could figure out who was coming and going in the area of the broken one, right?"

"Yup."

"Is there any way someone could get into the area not covered by the other cameras without being picked up by one of them?"

Ryan chewed his gingerbread slowly.

I had only the slightest bit of doubt that he didn't know where I was going with this, but the length of time he was taking to answer was starting to make me nervous. I glanced over at Sammy, who seemed to be awaiting Ryan's reply just as eagerly as I was, maybe more. My interest in this case wasn't personal—well, it was since Sammy had asked me to do it, but I didn't have a vested interest in it. Sammy, on the other hand—Ann Crowsdale was one of her heroes, and I knew she would be crushed if it turned out that she really had murdered Veronica Underwood.

Ryan finally swallowed. "Hypothetically?" he asked.

"Hypothetically," I confirmed.

"*Hypothetically*, depending on the location and the setup of the cameras, someone could get into the area covered only by the broken camera without being picked up by any of the functional cameras. That's why we tell people to have cameras covering the entire area."

"And have you ever seen a setup where this hypothetical situation would be possible?"

"I have," he said slowly.

"Recently?"

"Fran." His voice was reproachful. I was pushing my luck.

"Sorry."

"Nothing to be sorry about. I just have an active investigation I need to be thinking about." He paused. "And a boss who's been sort of temperamental lately."

I nodded. I couldn't blame him for not wanting to run afoul of Mike with the mood he'd been in lately.

He shoved the last of the gingerbread man into

his mouth and chewed it slowly. I assumed the conversation was over and started mentally debating more espresso. But Ryan eventually swallowed and had more to say. "The other thing is, Fran," he said gently, addressing me but looking at Sammy, "we take a lot of things into account before we make an arrest, especially in a murder case like this. One piece of evidence not being airtight doesn't mean the whole case falls apart."

Sammy looked down at the counter. Ryan looked as if he were in pain for a second and then turned away. I patted Sammy on the back.

"I know," I said. "It's just hard."

Ryan nodded.

Before the situation could get any more uncomfortable, the radio on Ryan's shoulder beeped, and some garbled nonsense started coming out of it. Ryan leaned toward it as if he could understand and then muttered something equally incoherent back into it.

"Looks like I gotta go," he said to us, speaking normal English again.

"Need some coffee for the road?" I asked.

"If you're buying," he said with a lopsided grin.

"Just this once," I joked back. I poured his cup of regular drip coffee then grabbed a second to-go cup. "Need another one?" I asked, both of us knowing I was asking about Mike.

"Has the answer ever been no?"

I poured the second cup of coffee but didn't mention Mike abandoning his cup of coffee the day before. Maybe Sammy told him. I wasn't going to bring it up.

I handed him both cups, and he headed for the door. "Thanks, Fran. Bye, Sammy."

I waved goodbye. Sammy was still staring at the counter.

"If you need a minute, there's still that napkin order to be placed," I said softly.

She looked at me in confusion then nodded when she realized I was offering her the same excuse to go take a minute in the back as she'd offered me the day before. "Thanks," she said and went in the back to cry.

Chapter 20

SAMMY MIGHT HAVE BEEN FEELING DISCOURAGED, but I wasn't ready to give in just yet. Yes, the police weighed lots of factors before making an arrest, and Ryan sounded every bit as confident about their suspect as Mike did, but I saw the heartbroken look on Sammy's face when Ryan said that one weak piece of evidence wasn't enough to ruin their case, and I couldn't just let the matter go until I knew I'd investigated every possible lead. And I still had leads to investigate.

Kristin had said that there was stuff I obviously didn't know about and that I wasn't used to dealing with "people like this." That I was getting into "dangerous stuff." I needed to know what that stuff was.

I wanted to go sit down at the laptop in the back and spend some more time digging around online, maybe this time doing some general searches instead of just looking at the social networks, but Sammy was back there and needed her peace. I pulled my phone out of my pocket instead. I'd barely unlocked it when the bell over the door jingled, and it really was the lunchtime rush.

I spent the next couple of hours steadily making drinks, serving sandwiches and snacks, and cleaning tables. Sammy came out of the back before too long, having cried herself out and calmed down, and Rhonda came in toward the end to work her shift. The crowd eventually cleared out, leaving just some of the all-day people who had been there before the rush and a couple new ones who had taken their places. I excused myself to go to the back, leaving the café under Sammy and Rhonda's watch for a little while.

I sat down at the computer and pulled up the browser to begin searching. I decided to start by looking up Veronica again. I tried to find some kind of information about her teaching record or credentials, but that was apparently not public information, so I switched gears and just did a general search. I didn't know what I was looking for —news articles about arrests for organized crime or something, maybe?—but whatever it was, I didn't find it. There was nothing to even point me in the general direction of the dangerous stuff and people Kristin had been talking about. So I looked up Kristin.

That took longer because I hadn't known about her to look at her social media accounts before, but it provided a wealth of interesting, though not obviously useful, information. For starters, Kristin worked as—of all things—a labor and delivery nurse. There were all kinds of public pictures of tired-looking people smiling with their new babies and Kristin, praising how wonderful of a nurse she was, how kind and patient, and what good care she took of them. I looked at the pictures that had Kristin smiling beside the parents and wondered who on earth this woman was.

Her friends list, full as it was with new parents, was prohibitively long to scroll through, but on the spur of the moment, and taking inspiration from Becky and her equally endless friend list, I clicked the button to send a friend request to Kristin. She'd probably say no, but on the off chance that she didn't, maybe I'd be able to find some more useful information.

I couldn't find any articles about Kristin being involved in organized crime, gambling rings, or anything else useful, seedy, or unseemly, so I switched over to searching for Gwen Blarney. I didn't really expect to find anything about her being involved in anything dangerous, and I wasn't surprised. I switched over to her social media profiles. We had a couple of friends in common, so I was able to see more on her page than I'd been able to on Kristin's, but there was still nothing that jumped out and announced that she had killed Veronica.

I clicked over to her friends list. It was less intimidatingly long, and there was a good chance that I knew some of the people since we both lived in Cape Bay, so I scrolled through the list. Aside from the people we already had in common, as I scrolled, I found a few people I'd known growing up who I hadn't quite reconnected with. In the spirit of being online friends with more people, I clicked the little plus sign next to their names too. I wasn't coming close to competing with Becky's friend count, but if all these people accepted me, I'd be working my way up to a more respectable number of friends.

Toward the end of the alphabetical-by-last-name list, I found a name that didn't quite surprise me but did interest me. Marcus Varros.

I clicked through to his page. He wisely had it

pretty locked down—maybe there was a course for principals in how to keep your students out of your private business, although if there was, there probably should have been one for teachers too, especially in light of what I'd been able to see on Veronica's page. Of course, from what I knew about Veronica, she probably would have done whatever she wanted even if she had been to a course on online privacy.

Varros's friend list was visible, though, so I clicked over to it and started scrolling. Gwen Blarney was toward the top in light of her last name being at the beginning of the alphabet, and I knew Veronica would be toward the end since her last name was Underwood. I was briefly surprised that he wasn't friends with Ann Crowsdale, but then again, that seemed as if it could be easily explained by her being arrested for murdering one of his other teachers. It probably wouldn't have looked good for him to still be friends with her, even if it was just online.

As I scrolled, I found a few more people whose plus signs I clicked. I wondered if I should start going through people's pages more often to see whom I knew that I'd overlooked.

By the time I got toward the middle of the longer-than-I-expected list, my eyes started to glaze over. I scrolled faster and paid less attention to the names. And then I thought I saw something that made me stop and scroll back up. My mouth fell open just a little as I saw the name. It wasn't a common name, but maybe it was common enough that there were two of them. I clicked on it and found out that, no, it was the same Kristin Mansmith.

I stared for a few seconds, wondering how they knew each other. Through Veronica? Something about that didn't seem right. Varros hadn't given any indication that he knew Kristin when he told me about her visit. And Kristin—I thought back to our conversation. There was something about it. And then I knew. When I told her about Varros's theory about her slashing the tires, she'd known his name without me telling her. And she sounded as if she was familiar with him.

Curious about something, I clicked back to his page and flipped over to the About section where it listed things like where he'd lived, where he'd gone to school, and who he was related to. Sure enough, it said he was from Providence. So maybe that was how he knew Kristin. I'd assumed he knew Veronica through the school, but maybe I was wrong about that. Mrs. Bayless and Mrs. Crawford had said that Veronica was hired very suddenly.

Maybe Varros knew her from back in Providence and that was why he hired her. But it didn't explain why she was hired so suddenly.

I looked back at Varros's page. He conveniently had his previous places of employment listed along with the dates he'd worked there. Until he'd been hired as the principal at Cape Bay High, he'd worked in the Providence public schools.

Before I could think any more about that, my cell phone rang. I dug it out of my pocket and saw that the call was from a number I didn't recognize. I nearly rejected the call, thinking it was probably a telemarketer or a scam artist trying to tell me I either owed the IRS a million dollars or had the once-in-a-lifetime opportunity to make a million dollars by helping a Nigerian prince sneak his money out of the country. For some reason, though, I hit the little green icon instead.

"Hello?" I asked cautiously.

"Hey, Fran!"

"Hi." I didn't recognize the voice, but he apparently recognized mine.

"How's it going?"

"Fine, and you?"

"Great! Hey, it was good to see you today!"

The voice was male, so I tried to think of the men I'd seen that day. Varros? No, it wasn't him. Ed from the Surfside? No, not him either. Ryan? Definitely not. "Brett?"

He laughed. "You didn't know it was me, did you?"

"No," I said slowly. I was confused, partly because he sounded so cheery and partly because, well, why on earth would Brett be calling me? How did he even get my number?

"I got your number from the school sign-in sheet when Mrs. B wasn't looking."

Had I asked that out loud? No, I was pretty sure I hadn't. And I didn't think Brett was a mind reader, but it was probably obvious that I was going to ask that next, so it hadn't been hard for him to guess.

"Anyway, I wanted to see if you could meet up tonight. I have my violin lesson at seven, so we could meet after it's over. Like at nine?"

I was so confused. Was Brett asking me out? It sounded like the inept way a teenage boy would ask someone out.

"I'm not asking you out or anything," he said, convincing me that he could actually hear my thoughts. "I just got a hold of some information I thought you might like to take a look at."

My curiosity was piqued. "Some information? What kind of information?"

"About Veronica's murder. What else would it be? I don't know what other kind of freaky stuff you're into."

Well, despite his new cheeriness, Brett was still Brett.

"So you want to meet up or not?"

I hesitated. Common sense told me I should say no, I would not meet up with this teenage boy whom I'd already been accused of harassing and warned to stay away from, but listening to common sense wouldn't have gotten me very far in this case or any other. "Sure. Where do you want to meet?"

"I dunno. How about your place?"

"My house?"

"Yeah. You don't have a house or something?"

"I do. I'm just not sure it's the best idea." To meet with any teenage boy in my house at nine o'clock at night, let alone this one.

"Then I could meet you here."

"Here? What do you mean, 'here'?"

"Hold on just a second." His voice got quieter, as if he was holding his phone away from his head, but I could still hear what he was saying. And he was distinctly ordering a latte and sugar cookies. "Sorry about that," he said at normal volume again.

I nearly got up and walked out into the café, but

this time I listened to the little voice screaming at me that Mike would have my head if he found out I was talking to Brett. And in the café, there were plenty of people who could potentially tell him. "Are you in the café?"

"Yeah, it's how I remembered to call you. So you wanna just meet here?"

If the café during the day was a bad idea, it would be just as bad at night when anyone would be able to look in through the wall of windows and see us inside. Unless we were in the back room... but that had the same deeply inappropriate vibe as meeting him at my house. "That's probably not a good idea either. Someone could see us and—"

He laughed. "Oh yeah, I heard my mom called and screamed at the police chief about that. What can I say? I'm her precious little angel." I heard him take a bite of something, and the next thing he said sounded as though his mouth was full—probably of one of my sugar cookies. "How about the park? It's dark. Probably no one there to see us, and if they do, whatever, people walk in parks and see other people all the time."

I thought about it. The park was still sketchy, but I was starting to accept the fact that there was no non-sketchy place to meet him. At least the park was public. And I could always bring Latte. And

Matt. But Brett might not talk if Matt was around. So maybe Matt could hide… I shut my brain off. I was overthinking it and making a bad idea worse. "Sure, let's meet at the park."

"Awesome. Park, nine. Down by the pond, okay?"

"Okay," I said and then realized he'd already disconnected the call. For a second, I just sat there and stared at my phone, wondering just what I was getting myself into.

Chapter 21

"WHAT ARE you getting yourself into, Franny?" Matt asked later that afternoon when I told him about my meeting with Brett. "You're planning to meet with a teenage boy—who is at best unpredictable and at worst dangerous—in the park after dark, supposedly to get information about a murder investigation that the police have already solved. What about that sounds like a good idea?"

"Getting information about a murder investigation," I said.

"None of it, Franny. The right answer is none of it." He shook his head and tapped his coffee cup on the table in the back room of the café. "You know I'm going with you, right?"

"I don't think Brett will talk if you're with me."

"You don't think Brett will…" he muttered and shook his head again. "You realize how ridiculous that sounds, don't you?"

"Brett trusts me."

"He trusts you? How do you know that? And why would he? You've met him once!"

"Three times, if you count the times in the principal's office."

"Franny…" He shook his head and took a sip of his coffee. From his tone, I couldn't tell if he was really mad at me for planning to meet up with Brett or just mystified as to why I thought it was a good idea. "I'm going with you," he said again.

"Only if you don't let Brett see you." Even to my ears, it sounded genuinely crazy.

"Only if I don't—Franny, if I'm hidden away somewhere and he tries to hurt you, I'm not going to be able to help you. If he has a gun, he could shoot you before I even see it."

"I have no reason to think he's going to try to shoot me. He sounded perfectly pleasant when I talked to him earlier."

Matt looked me dead in the eye. "And has he ever sounded perfectly pleasant when you've talked to him before?"

"Well, no."

"So what makes you think this is a good idea?

What makes you think he doesn't have some ulterior motive to want to get you alone? You really believe that he, of all people, has some inside information that you haven't been able to get anywhere else?"

"Actually, *that* I believe. You haven't met Brett. If anyone was going to have inside information, it would be him."

Matt looked at me skeptically.

"The kid's a literal genius. Off the charts IQ."

He didn't budge.

"Trust me, if you met him, you'd understand."

"Well, that's good, because I'll be meeting him tonight."

"Matty, please." I actually folded my hands in front of my chest but fell short of falling to my knees to beg him. "You can come with me, but please don't let Brett see you. Please."

"You could get hurt, Franny."

"I know."

"This could be a setup to get you alone."

"I know."

"He could have murdered that teacher, and you're the closest to catching him, so he's going to get you alone and kill you too."

"I know."

"And you're okay with that?"

"Well, no, but—Matty, I'm running out of leads. If Brett has information that could expose the real murderer, it's my civic duty to go get it."

"I think it would be your civic duty to tell the police about it and get him to give it to them."

"That's what I'm going to do."

Matt raised his eyebrows.

"Just indirectly. I'm going to get him to give it to me, and then, if it's any good, I'll give it to them."

"You're hopeless, Franny."

"I know. But you love me."

"I do." He opened his arms, and I stepped into them to let him hold me.

"Oops! Don't mind me!" Sammy said, coming into the room.

Matt dropped his arms, and I turned to her. "Headed out?" I asked.

"Yup. We're running a little low on the snowflake sugar cookies if you can make some more of them tonight."

I grimaced—inwardly, I hoped. I'd have to start them immediately if I was going to have them cooked and ready to be iced before I went to meet Brett, and even then it would be cutting it close. Really close.

"If you can just have the sheets ready, I can just

pop them in the oven in the morning. People love the smell of freshly baked cookies."

"Good idea. I'll have the sheets ready and waiting in the refrigerator."

"Perfect!" She slipped her coat on, flipped her long blond ponytail out from inside it, and put her bag on her shoulder. "I'll see you tomorrow then!"

"Oh, hey!"

She stopped and turned around.

"Did that Cheryl girl show up today? The creepy one?"

"Ryan's ex-girlfriend? You can say it, Fran. We've both dated other people before."

"Okay, yes, Ryan's ex-girlfriend. Did she show up today?"

"Nope. I think you scared her off."

"Great! Well, have a good night."

"You too."

"What's this about you scaring people off?" Matt asked when Sammy was gone.

I hadn't told him about Cheryl? The murder investigation had been taking up more of my brain than I realized. "It's a long story," I said.

"Involving Ryan's creepy ex-girlfriend?"

"Yup," I said as I started piling my baking supplies in my arms for the sugar cookies.

"And why is she coming here?"

"That's the long story. I'll tell you about it later. Could you grab the butter for me? And my mixing bowls?"

Matt sighed but got up to help me with my supplies. Then he helped me mix the cookie dough. It was cute and domestic, and he only ended up with a light dusting of flour covering virtually his entire body.

"I can't take you anywhere," I said as I stood back and appraised his flour-covered body.

"How are you so clean?" he asked.

"Practice." I tapped the particularly heavy concentration of flour on his nose in lieu of ruffling his newly white hair—I didn't want to get hair in the cookies. "You should go home and get a shower."

"Are you coming with me?" he grinned.

"Ooh, maybe." I moved closer to him, but not too close, because I didn't want to get flour all over myself. My eye caught the clock on the wall, and I realized that it was almost time to go. "Actually, no."

"No?" He looked disappointed.

I pointed at the big wrought iron clock. "We need to clean up so I can be on time to meet Brett."

"Haven't given that up yet, huh?"

"And I'm not going to. He has important information. I can feel it."

"If you say so," Matt said and started helping me get the trays of uncooked snowflake-shaped sugar cookies into the refrigerator.

We finished getting everything cleaned up. I would have just enough time to get home, get Latte, and get to the park. With flour-covered Matt in tow, of course.

———

THIRTY MINUTES LATER, Latte and I were nearing the pond in the park. It wasn't that late, but at that time of year, darkness came early. I knew the path wasn't well lit, so I'd brought a flashlight along. I figured it would also prove useful if Brett had some documents to show me. The moon was full and bright enough that I hadn't turned it on, though. Despite that, and even with Matt trailing behind me, it still felt sort of spooky walking through the park in the dark.

As I reached the pond, I saw a figure standing on the opposite side. In the dark, I couldn't see its features, but I knew it could only be one person. Brett. Still, on the off chance it wasn't, I didn't call out to him. I just turned off the main path and started along the part that looped around the pond. Matt and I had agreed that he'd hide behind a tree near the intersection of the two paths and watch my meeting from there. Well, I agreed that he'd hide behind a tree. All he agreed to was to stay at the intersection, and even *that* I wasn't terribly confident about him actually doing. But as long as he stayed out of sight and didn't ruin my rendezvous, I didn't care. I did wonder if it was a bad idea to call meeting up with a teenager a rendezvous, though.

I watched the figure as I circled the pond, hoping that he'd turn and the light would hit his face so that I could be sure it was Brett. It was eerie approaching him without being sure. The figure stayed mostly in one place but walked in little circles. He—I was almost certain it was a he—seemed to be following my approach, which was either a really good sign or a really bad sign.

Finally, I was close enough that I could speak to him and he could hear me without me having to shout. Shouting seemed like a bad idea given the clandestine nature of our meeting. I still wasn't one hundred percent sure it was Brett, but who else could it be?

"Brett?" I called cautiously and not very loudly.

No response.

I walked a few steps closer. "Brett?" I said again but more quietly.

The figure sighed. "I was afraid it was you," it said, but the voice wasn't Brett's. It was—

"Mike." I felt nauseous. Was this a setup? Had Brett set me up? Or maybe it was just a coincidence. I tried to sound cheerful and like nothing unusual was going on. "I didn't expect to run into you here! How's it going? I haven't seen you in a couple of days!"

"I know you didn't expect to run into me here. You expected to run into Brett."

"Brett? Brett who?"

"Don't play dumb with me, Francesca." He took a step closer to me, close enough now that I could see his face in the moonlight. He did not look happy. And he was using my full name again. Not a good sign. Also not a good sign that he knew I was supposed to meet Brett. The little brat really had set me up.

"Oh, you mean Brett Wallace?"

"Are there any other Bretts you've been harassing lately to the point that they'd rather kill themselves than meet up with you again?"

All the air was suddenly gone from my lungs. My mouth tried to form words, but there was no air to push them out. After what seemed like an eternity, I finally managed to get out a single weak "what?"

"Don't worry. He's not dead. At least I assume you're not messed up enough to want him dead. I'm not sure I know anymore."

I could breathe again, at least a little. "He's not —he's not—"

"Nope, he's not dead. He tried, though."

I finally managed a complete sentence. "What happened?"

"He drove himself into a light pole on his way home from his violin lesson. At least, he was supposed to be on his way home. According to his phone, he was on his way to meet you."

To meet me. Brett drove himself into a light pole on his way to meet me. "But he's the one who asked me to meet him."

"Geez, don't lie to me, Fran. At least give me that much respect."

"I'm not lying! You can check my phone! He called me!" I reached into my pocket to pull it out and show him.

"Keep your hands where they are!" Mike's hand dropped to his hip, and I slowly moved mine away from my pocket and up beside my face.

"I don't—I'm not—"

"I can't believe I'm doing this," he muttered, walking over to me. He patted the pockets on both sides of my coat and then my jeans.

"Mike, you don't think—"

"I don't know what to think anymore, Franny." He took a couple steps back away from me, as if he didn't want to be near me. He stood there and stared at me for a long time.

"I didn't ask Brett to meet me here," I said finally in a voice barely above a whisper.

"But you're here. After I asked you to stay away."

"I know, I—" Mike shook his head ever so slightly, and I stopped. No excuse or explanation would make a difference now. "Is Brett going to be okay?"

"Should be. He lost consciousness for a little while, and they have him sedated now, but they think he'll be okay. We should know more tomorrow."

I nodded. "Please, if you see his family, tell them I—"

He raised a hand to stop me. "I don't think they want to hear anything from you. His mother's already been on the phone with the chief, trying to get you arrested for harassment."

"But I haven't been—"

"It doesn't matter, Franny."

I stared down at Latte, who was uncharacteristi-cally sitting quietly by my side.

"I better go. Sandra's waiting. I already missed tucking the kids into bed." He stared at me for a few seconds then sighed resolutely. "Take care, Fran." He turned around and walked a few steps before pausing to call back over his shoulder. "And tell Matt he can come out from behind the trees. He's not as hidden as he thinks he is." He walked away without turning back again.

I stared after him until I felt Matt's hand on my shoulder. "What happened?" he asked.

"Brett was in a car accident. Mike said—" I choked back a sob. "Mike said he tried to kill himself."

Matt pulled me in to him, and I let him, flour and all. "It's not your fault, Franny."

I nodded as though I agreed, but I knew that it was.

Chapter 22

I WOKE up the next morning feeling broken inside, and it took me a few minutes to figure out why. When I did, I seriously considered going back to sleep. Before I could, Latte noticed me and crawled over to kiss me all over my face. It's hard to fall asleep when you have a dog actively applying his slobber to you.

"All right, all right." I rolled over and sat up on the edge of the bed. Latte, not dissuaded in the slightest, shoved his head under my arm and nuzzled me frantically. "Hungry?" Latte leapt from the bed and raced to my bedroom door. I got up and stumbled after him. Downstairs—I still hadn't gotten myself moved into the first-floor master—I scooped his food and started myself a cup of coffee.

Then I sat at the kitchen table and stared into space while Latte ate. When he was done, I let him out the back door and left it cracked so he could push it open when he was ready to come in. I shivered from the chill as the icy air blew in.

For a brief second, I wondered if maybe Brett hadn't driven into the light pole on purpose. Maybe he'd hit a patch of ice and skidded there. Maybe it was an accident. Maybe it wasn't my fault. But then I remembered stepping over a puddle on my way home from the park last night and realized it hadn't been cold enough when he crashed for there to have been a patch of ice.

I sat back down at the table and stared while I waited for Latte to come back in. When he did, I closed the door and went through the motions of my morning—eating, showering, getting dressed, blow-drying my hair so I didn't end up with a frozen helmet when I went outside on my long, cold walk with Latte.

And it was a long walk, longer than usual. Instead of our usual lap around the neighborhood, we wandered aimlessly through town. At each intersection, I let Latte lead us in whichever direction most appealed to his nose. Apparently that was the direction of salty sea air, because I eventually found myself standing on the beach.

I had always loved the beach, but of course, who didn't? Still, having grown up in Cape Bay, with the crash of the waves the soundtrack of my childhood and the salt air its perfume, being on the beach gave me a peace it was hard to feel anywhere else.

Latte and I were the only ones on the beach, so I unhooked his leash and flung his tennis ball. He took off after it. I shoved my hands in my pockets and stared at the waves. If it hadn't been barely above freezing temperatures, I would have taken my shoes off, rolled up my jeans, and let the water sink my feet into the sand. But I liked having toes and didn't want to lose them to wading-induced frostbite, so I kept my boots on.

Latte brought his ball back, and I threw it again. And again. And again. And again until Latte was exhausted and dropped himself in addition to his ball at my feet. I wouldn't say I was feeling good by then, but I was feeling better, as if I could handle facing customers and making coffee instead of just sitting and staring into space. I hooked Latte's leash back up to his collar and headed first for home and then for the café.

What I saw when I walked in wasn't what I expected.

Sammy was standing at the counter, which

wasn't unusual, but her tight-lipped expression and hands clutching its edge were. For a split second, I was afraid we were being robbed, even though there was no one standing across from her. But when I followed her gaze to the group sitting across from her, I realized what was wrong.

"I thought I told you not to come back here," I said, singling Ryan's ex Cheryl out in what I assumed was her group of friends. Apparently I had not been as effective in scaring her off as I'd thought.

"You did?" she asked, looking at me blankly and innocently, as if I hadn't physically escorted her from the café just two days before. "I don't think you said that."

I tried to think back to whether those words had literally come out of my mouth. It was possible that they hadn't, but shouldn't escorting her out have been enough? It would have been for anyone else, but apparently Cheryl's level of crazy ran even deeper than I'd thought.

"Well, I meant to. You need to leave. Now. All of you." I looked dead into her eyes. "And don't come back."

Cheryl looked at me for a second and then leaned back in her chair, hooking her arms over the back. "No." She looked at me defiantly. "This is a public place, and I have a right to be here."

"That's where you're wrong. This is private property, and I have the right to refuse service to anyone who is here just to harass my employees."

"Who, me? Harassing? I'm not harassing anyone! Me and my friends here are just enjoying a nice cup of coffee and some cookies."

Most of them did have coffee cups in front of them. I admired Sammy for that. Knowing her, she would have been friendly and pleasant while serving them, even if what she really wanted to do was throw the cups at their heads.

And there was a plate of cookies in the middle of the table. Cheryl was actually picking one up at that moment.

"So, see? We're not harassing anyone." She smiled and looked at the gingerbread woman in her hand. It had long blond hair, a pink smile, and blue eyes. It was a cookie that I suspected Sammy had designed to look like herself, and I remembered seeing how she'd arranged it in the display case next to the smiling police officer cookie, almost as though they were holding hands. Cheryl looked from the cookie to Sammy, still smiling, then snapped the gingerbread woman's head off. She tossed it on the table and bit into the spot on the cookie where it had been.

"That's it. Get out!" I spoke a little too loudly, drawing the attention of everyone in the café who hadn't already been watching the confrontation. I walked over to the group, stopping just short of Cheryl. I wanted to grab her by the arm and drag her out, but I didn't think that would be wise.

Cheryl looked at one of her friends, the one closest to her. "This is that girl I told you about. The one who *assaulted* me," she said loudly so that everyone in the café could hear. She even looked around at all of them as though they were her audience and she wanted to make sure she had their attention.

I took a step closer, so I was standing over her. "I did not assault you, and you know it. Now get out, and take all your friends with you."

"No."

I clenched my jaw. "Get out now, or I will call the police."

"For what? Being paying customers?"

"For trespassing and harassing my employee."

She took another bite of gingerbread. Her friends, as if on command, all took bites of their own cookies or sipped their cups of coffee.

"This is your last chance. Leave, or I call the police."

She didn't move.

"Sammy?" I held my hand out, operating on faith that she had released her white-knuckled grip on the counter and would be quick enough on her feet to slap the cordless phone into my palm. Thank goodness, she did.

I dialed the nine and one then looked at Cheryl as I hovered my finger over the one for the second time. "Last chance," I said.

She didn't even flinch.

I pushed the one button again and held the phone to my ear.

"Nine-one-one, what is your emergency?"

"Hi, this is Francesca Amaro down at Antonia's. I have some people trespassing here. I've asked them to leave, and they've refused."

One of Cheryl's friends, looking worried, looked around at the other ones, but none of them acknowledged her.

"Are they armed?" the 9-1-1 operator asked.

Well, there were no guns or hunting knives sitting out on the table, but it wouldn't surprise me if this group had them tucked away in their purses. Still, I didn't think I could tell the dispatcher that.

"Not as far as I know," I said, feeling slightly foolish, as if this was a stupid reason to call the police.

I heard typing on the other end of the line. "And are they threatening you in any way?"

Did snapping off the head of a gingerbread woman that looked like my employee count? I didn't think so. "Not at the moment."

More typing. At that point, I was just waiting for her to tell me that this wasn't something I should have called the police for and hang up on me. Fortunately, she didn't.

"Okay, Fran, I've dispatched an officer on a nonemergency trespassing call to your location. He's nearby, so he should be there in just a few minutes. Would you like me to stay on the line with you until he arrives?"

I declined. What would I do if I stayed on the line with her, anyway? Ask her about her day? Invite her down for coffee after work? Actually, that wasn't too bad of an idea.

She stopped me before I could suggest it, though. "If anything changes about your situation before he gets there, please let me know so I can update the responding officer."

"Thanks, I will." Just before I hung up, I got a slightly panicky feeling. "What's the name of the officer who's coming?" I wasn't sure I was ready to face Mike if he was the one coming. And not that I doubted his professionalism for a second, but I wasn't exactly sure he'd be thrilled to handle a nonemergency call from me either. At least Sammy was still on his good side, and she was the one who really needed his help, even if it was my property that was being trespassed on.

"The officer is Ryan Leary," the dispatcher said.

I breathed a sigh of relief before I remembered that he was the reason Cheryl was harassing Sammy. Still, it was better than having to face Mike. I thanked the dispatcher and hung up the phone.

"The police are on their way," I announced, making sure I said it loud enough for the whole café to hear so that they knew this wasn't just some childish spat. Of course, there was also the chance that they would interpret it to mean that I didn't hesitate to call the police on my customers, but I figured most of them knew me well enough to know that wasn't the case.

"Good," Cheryl said, adjusting her position in her chair but not looking any more as though she was getting ready to leave. "Maybe I can talk to them about that assault charge."

"Be my guest." I gave her a smile that wasn't even meant to look sincere then turned my back on her and walked around the counter to where

Sammy had retreated after giving me the phone. She was now white-knuckle clutching the other side of the counter. I dropped the phone into its charger. "You can go in the back," I said, not bothering with any napkin-ordering pretenses.

Wordlessly, she went into the storage room and shut the door behind her.

I stood there and wondered what was taking Ryan so long before I realized that it hadn't even been a full minute since I hung up the phone. Still, Cape Bay wasn't *that* big.

To keep myself calm, I walked around the counter and went up to the first customer who wasn't Cheryl or her friends. "I'm so sorry for all the—" I waved my hand in the direction of Cheryl's posse. "Unpleasantness. Can I get you a free refill of your drink or perhaps some complimentary cookies?"

They took me up on it, because my customers were generally well behaved, but not stupid, and I worked my way around the café, doing my best to ingratiate myself to my customers and prove to them that I was the good guy in this situation. I had just taken care of the last customer—except Cheryl's table, of course—when Ryan and another officer came in. It was all I could do to keep myself from asking what had taken them so long.

Just inside the door, Ryan said something quietly to the other officer and pointed in Cheryl's direction then came over to me. The other officer moved toward her but stopped before he got too close.

"Cheryl?" Ryan asked.

I nodded, then he turned to the other officer and nodded. That officer walked the rest of the way over to the table.

"A'right, ladies, let's go," he said.

The one who had looked nervous earlier made a move to get up, but none of the rest of them did. She sank back down into her chair.

"I said, let's go!"

None of them moved.

Ryan put his hand on my shoulder and turned me around, leading me a few steps farther away from the group. "Sorry it took me so long to get here," he said, low enough that only I could hear. "I had a feeling I knew what was going on and thought I should bring some backup."

I nodded and nearly thanked him for not choosing to bring Mike. But for all I knew, maybe he'd tried to bring him and Mike had declined.

"Is Sam okay?"

I nodded again. "She's in the back. I don't think they really said anything to her, but I haven't had a chance to talk to her. I just got here."

Now Ryan nodded. "We're going to get them out of here and take their statements, then I'll come back and get yours." He took a deep breath. "In the meantime, could you go check on Sammy?"

I glanced around at my customers scattered throughout the café. They'd all gotten fresh food and drinks, but I didn't really want to go shut myself off in the back room in case they needed anything.

Ryan, apparently reading my mind, grinned. "Maybe after the entertainment's over, they'll need some refreshments, but I think they'll be fine for now."

He had a point. I headed for the back room. Cheryl muttered a swear word at me as I walked by. I bristled but did my best to ignore it. Just as I got to the back room, I heard Ryan talking to the women behind me. "Okay, everybody who doesn't want to add to their arrest record, stand up and step outside so we can take your statement. Everybody who doesn't mind spending the night in the Cape Bay jail, stay where you are."

I slipped into the back room before I could hear anything else and closed the door again behind me.

Sammy looked up at me from where she was slumped in the chair by the computer. "I'm so sorry, Fran."

"For what?"

"It's my fault they're here."

"Unless you invited them, I don't think it is."

She looked at me solemnly and then looked down. "They're still here because of me."

"They're here because of their own bad decisions. Because of some weird game of follow-the-leader. They didn't even get up when the police told them to. Ryan was threatening to arrest them when I came back here."

"Ryan's here?"

I nodded.

She looked even more miserable. "It's so embarrassing."

I pulled a chair up next to her. "Why's it embarrassing? You're not the one showing up at someone's workplace, making a fool of yourself."

She sighed and stared at her fingernails. I patted her on the back. I understood.

"I think she's stalking me," she said after a long while, during which I could hear muffled voices out in the café but, thankfully, couldn't understand a word of what they were saying.

"I think that's fair," I replied. It might be a hard sell to get the police to do anything about it after just a few times of showing up at her place of work, but I didn't think she was wrong to call it stalking.

"I think she followed me home last night."

"What?" My voice came out louder than I meant it to, but I was stunned by what she'd just said.

"I kept thinking I heard footsteps behind me, but when I turned around, there was no one there."

"Are you serious?" I asked, even though I knew she was. Sammy wouldn't make up something like that.

She nodded. "And I've been getting a lot of email from places I didn't sign up to get email from."

"That happens sometimes. They sell your email address."

"I know, but I've been getting a lot of spam lately too. I know that's not that weird, but these are coming through to my inbox. And they have my name. They always say 'Sammy' in the subject or in the email." She looked at me, and I could see the fear in her eyes. "Do you get spam that has your name in it?"

I tried to think. I didn't think so, but I really didn't know. I didn't usually pay that much attention to my spam folder except to make sure there weren't any emails about good sales that mistakenly got sent there. "I'm not really sure."

"Me neither. I don't know if my mind is playing tricks on me, or if she's doing something."

"Have you told Ryan about any of this?"

She shook her head. "No. It would just make me sound crazy and jealous."

"Ryan wouldn't think that." At least, I didn't think so. Cheryl certainly seemed crazy enough to make Sammy's story believable. But maybe Ryan had a habit of dating crazy girls and wouldn't realize that Sammy wasn't. "What about Mike?"

"I thought about it, but—" She glanced at me then looked down and shrugged.

"But what?" I asked. "He's here all the time. You could just mention it to him and see what he thinks."

She didn't say anything.

"Sammy?"

Her eyes flicked up at me and then back down. "He hasn't been in," she said softly.

I thought I heard her wrong. "He hasn't—" I stopped. "At all? Since Tuesday?"

She shook her head, and I sank down in my chair. I felt sick. Mike usually came in at least twice a day. If we only saw him once, I wondered if something was wrong. And he hadn't been in at all in two days.

We sat there in glum silence until my phone

dinged to alert me to a text message. I pulled it out of my pocket and looked at it. For a second, my heart stopped.

It was from Brett.

He wanted me to come see him.

Chapter 23

AFTER A LENGTHY INTERNAL DEBATE, and
then another one with Brett about how it was a
really bad idea for me to go see him in the hospital,
and then another with Matt about how mad Mike
would be when he found out—because he
inevitably would—I went. I wasn't sure why, but I
was pretty sure it was to apologize for—for what?
For driving him to attempt suicide by accusing him
of maybe murdering his teacher? Showing up in his
hospital room seemed like an awful way to apologize for that. Going away forever seemed like a
much better way to do it. But Brett was insistent
and, I was pretty sure, quite used to getting what he
wanted. So I went to the hospital.

I showed up the next day—around lunchtime,

when Brett assured me his mother would be out lunching with her friends. Even with his assurances, after signing in, I practically crept down the hall, ready at any minute to jump into a room if I saw anyone not in nurses' scrubs approaching. And then, when I got to his room, I stood outside for a long while, making sure the only noise I heard inside was the television. Finally, when I had more or less convinced myself it was safe, I knocked.

"Come in!" The voice that called out sounded like Brett's, but I still hesitated. "I said, come in!" it yelled again, louder this time. "Don't make me come to the door; I'm an invalid!"

Had Brett really just used the word "invalid"? This kid really was weird. I opened the door.

"Fran!" He smiled broadly when he saw me. "Did you bring me some cookies?"

"And cocoa," I said, holding up the drink carrier. The other drink it held was a latte, but that was for me.

"Cocoa?" He wrinkled his nose. "I'm sixteen, not six."

"Too much caffeine isn't good for a boy your age," I said, handing it to him. I realized I probably sounded old and uncool to his ears but decided I didn't care. I was way too old to care what the popular kids thought of me.

"What's in the other one?"

"More cocoa," I fudged.

His eyes narrowed. "Liar." He sipped his cocoa. "But this is good."

I handed over the bag of cookies. He looked through it carefully before pulling out one of Sammy's sparkling snowflakes. A good choice.

I sat down in the chair beside his bed as he munched on the cookie. Despite the sound of the TV and his chewing, the room was too quiet for me. "I'm sorry," I said in an attempt to ease my discomfort.

He made a face.

"For, you know, making you want to, uh, um—" I couldn't bring myself to say the words.

"Kill myself?"

"Uh-huh," I said, feeling even more uncomfortable than before I'd spoken up.

"You think that's what happened too? Why does everybody think I was trying to off myself? Do I seem like I want to die?" He took another bite of the cookie.

"No, um, well, yes, um—" I couldn't put two words together. I tried to remember what I'd seen on some morning show about talking to depressed teens.

"I didn't drive into that light pole on purpose."

"You didn't? But Mike—I mean, the police said—"

"Yeah, yeah, that's what the cops are telling everybody. But it wasn't on purpose."

"Distracted driving then?" I asked, more relieved than I should have been by the thought of a teenager not paying attention to the road.

"Try road rage."

"You drove into the light pole because you were angry?"

He rolled his eyes the way only teenagers can. "No, Fran! I drove into the light pole because *someone else* was angry! He pushed me into it."

"He did? Someone pushed you? Why? What did you do?"

"It's always the teenager's fault, huh? You're such an adult. I thought you were cooler than that, Fran."

For a second, I found myself inordinately pleased that Brett thought I was cool, but then I remembered that he was less than half my age and I wasn't in high school anymore. But regardless of that, he was telling me that someone had intentionally driven him off the road. "Okay, so why was this guy so angry that he drove you off the road?"

"Because of what I know."

"Because of what you know?" I hadn't thought

about it before, but he must have gotten a concussion from the accident. He was delusional.

"Yup." He bit into the cookie.

I knew I shouldn't ask it, but I did. "And what is it that you know?" I took a sip of my latte as I waited for his answer. That we didn't really land on the moon, maybe. That lizard people were secretly running the world. That an espresso would magically go bad after ten seconds.

"Why Veronica Underwood was murdered."

I barely kept from spitting my latte all over him. "What?" I managed to get out as I coughed out the coffee I'd inhaled.

"I know why Veronica Underwood was murdered," he repeated.

Because she was an awful person? Because someone had finally gotten sick of her attitude? Because she was into something dangerous involving people I wasn't used to dealing with?

"Well, not exactly why, but it has something to do with it."

Figures. Brett was just screwing with me again.

"Take a look at this." Brett held out his phone for me to look at.

It was a picture of a document with Veronica Underwood's name at the top. I quickly tried to skim its contents, but it was too small. I reached out to take the phone from Brett so I could enlarge it, but he pulled it back.

"Know what that is?" he asked.

I shook my head.

"Veronica's teaching certificate. Well," he scoffed, "her lack thereof."

My forehead wrinkled in confusion.

Brett swiped at his phone. "That came with this." He held out his phone again. All I could tell was that it was a letter. I thought I saw the name Varros on it, but he turned it away again before I could be sure. He swiped again. "And then there's this." It was a printed-out email. "And this." Did that say Marcus? "And this." A check? "And this." It looked like another email, but Brett turned it around again before I could be sure.

"Stop that!" I snapped, fed up with him flashing the pictures at me faster than I could comprehend them. I tried to grab his phone, but he was quicker than me and pulled it away.

He laughed.

"Stop being a brat and just tell me whatever it is you're trying to tell me." I wanted to call him another name, but on the off chance he was actually trying to share some valuable information with me, I didn't want to alienate him. Of course, knowing him, he probably would have respected me more and been more willing to share whatever information it was he claimed to have.

But as it was, he laughed again.

I leaned back in the chair and crossed my arms across my chest.

"Aw, come on, Fran! Don't get mad!" He was still laughing.

"I'm not mad," I said, even though I knew I probably should have just kept my mouth shut. "I'm just done playing your little games."

"But games are fun!"

I rolled my eyes and sipped my latte. I considered telling him that was what it was, but I was pretty sure he already knew. Letting him know that he was right would just feed his little ego.

"C'mon, Fran!" he said again.

I ignored him as I relished the rich flavor of my latte.

"Oh, all right!"

I looked at him skeptically and waited.

"Look, I don't know all the details, but Veronica shouldn't have been allowed to teach."

I raised my eyebrows.

"That one letter I showed you—" He scrolled through his phone and pulled up the letter that I'd thought I saw Varros's name on. "It's from the Rhode Island Department of Education to Varros.

It says that her Rhode Island teacher's certificate had been revoked because all her records were faked, and tells him he should check on it."

Interesting, but I didn't see why it was reason to kill her. I'd never heard of someone being that furious over a falsified resume. Unless... I sat up. "What do the other documents say?"

Brett grinned. I could tell he was happy he'd piqued my interest. "Well, one's a check, and the rest are emails."

"What do they say?"

"They're mostly between Veronica and Varros. I saw Blarney's name on a couple of them. I didn't get to read them all, though. I had a test and then play practice and then violin, and then, well—" He gestured at the hospital bed. "I got put up in this place. It's not bad, though. The bed's comfortable, and the food's better than you'd think. Not much on TV, but I watch everything on here anyway." He wiggled his phone in his hand.

"Where did you get these pictures?" I asked.

"I took them."

I took a deep breath, trying to control my temper. "Where did you take them?"

"Just wherever I was. In between classes."

"Brett!"

He laughed again. It was annoying. "I pulled

the folder with all the papers in it from Varros's office and then took the pictures during my classes. I had a feeling I'd need a backup."

"Where are the papers now?"

He shrugged. "Dunno. They were in my bag when I was on my way to see you, but they're not there now. I figure he took them when I was passed out."

Part of me already knew the answer, but I had to ask the question anyway. "Who is 'he,' Brett?"

He smirked. "You know."

"Brett!" I fully realized I sounded like a parent about to lose their patience.

"It's Varros. He's the only one who could have known I had the papers. Didn't know I had a copy, though." He waggled his phone again.

If Brett was right—if Varros had run him off the road in order to take back the documents Brett had stolen—then this might be exactly the break in the case I was looking for. On the other hand, he might be wrong. Or he might be lying just to get a reaction from me. With Brett, it was entirely possible. I had to see the pictures for myself.

"Can you send me a copy of those?" I asked.

He smirked again. "I already uploaded them to a secure site where they can't be hacked or deleted." He told me the name of it and gave me my username, which was just my name, somewhat disturbingly including my middle one. I didn't know how he got that, and I wasn't sure I wanted to. Then he rattled off a series of letters and numbers that were supposed to be my password.

"Hold on," I said. "Let me write that down."

"You can't write it down! Then it won't be secure."

"Brett, there's no way I'm going to remember all that."

"Why not? It's just an alphanumeric Fibonacci sequence using the letters of your name for a Caesar cipher. I mean, it's barely secure as it is."

I stared at him blankly.

He sighed. "Fine, I'll change it."

He picked up his phone and started tapping again, but the door flew open before he could finish.

"Bretty!" A woman's voice called out.

I froze.

"I brought you some lunch. And I have good news! I talked to the nurse, and she said you can come home today. So you'll still be able to go to your little play."

I turned around slowly, afraid of who I was going to see. Sure enough, it was an immaculately coiffed blond woman.

"Hi, Mom!" Brett said.

I sat completely still, hoping she was one of those predators who could only see movement.

Apparently not. "Who is this?" she asked, laying eyes on me.

"Oh, she's just a social worker," Brett said without hesitation. "She was worried that an unstable home life contributed to my accident."

I looked at him, wide eyed. The last thing I needed was for his mother to think I was trying to take custody away from her.

"But I assured her it wasn't, and she was just on her way out."

"Yes, I was," I said, standing up. Despite myself, I was grateful to Brett for providing me an easy exit. "Thank you, Brett, for your time. And it's a pleasure to meet you, Mrs. Wallace." I shook both their hands in as official a manner as I could manage and made my escape.

Chapter 24

BEFORE I WAS EVEN OUT of the hospital, Brett had texted me with a new password to use to access the documents he'd gotten from Varros's office. My plan had already been to head straight to the café since I needed my car there to load up for the play's opening night that evening, and now I was just hoping I could find some time to squeeze in a review of the documents. It was going to be tight with all the last-minute baking and packing Sammy and I needed to do. We were already closing the café early so we could get everything taken care of and then get over to the school to get set up before the doors opened.

I parked my car in the lot behind the café and headed for the back door. Inside, Sammy already had boxes of supplies piled high—plates, cups, napkins, plastic wrap, to-go boxes, jugs of water, a variety of freshly roasted, freshly ground coffees, and the small, somewhat portable espresso machine we used for occasions like this. I looked at it all and wondered if Sammy would have to go get her car too. I wasn't sure it would all fit in mine.

"Oh, Fran, thank goodness!" Sammy said, coming into the back room. "I need your help! It's crazy out there." She grabbed a pile of napkins and disappeared again.

I sighed as I put down my handbag and took off my coat. Brett's documents would have to wait until later. Much later, as it turned out. The café was unusually busy all day, and between taking care of customers, mixing, baking, and decorating fresh batches of cookies, and getting everything organized and loaded into my car—it did all fit, but just barely, with Sammy holding several trays of cookies and other baked goods on her lap—I didn't have a minute to spare the entire day.

"I heard Mrs. Crowsdale—I mean Ann—is going to be at the play tonight. In the audience, I mean. They're not letting her participate since the school system suspended her until the case is resolved," Sammy said as we drove over to the high school.

"Oh, that's great!" I replied. "Well, I guess. It'll probably be really hard for her too. Putting in all that work all year and then having to sit in the audience during the performance."

"I know. I feel so bad for her."

"In more ways than one."

"Have you made any progress on the case?"

I thought about it. Had I? I'd certainly worked on it enough, done enough research, talked to enough people. I had some ideas, but I really didn't know if they were worth anything. I had suspects, but I wasn't really sure which of them was the most likely culprit. I almost felt as if all my efforts had been for nothing. Almost, but not quite. After all, all my suspects were going to be at the play that night—Principal Varros, Gwen Blarney, Brett Wallace, even Ann Crowsdale. If only I had a library I could draw them all into for an Agatha Christie-style dramatic reveal. Of course, to do a reveal, I'd have to know whodunit.

"Fran?" Sammy said, making me realize I'd been lost in my thoughts about the case. "Have you made any progress?"

"I'm not sure," I admitted as I turned into the school parking lot. "But maybe."

We spent the next hour and a half or so getting our tables set up and decorated in true Christmassy fashion. As I stepped back to admire what was, admittedly, mostly Sammy's work turning the tables into a red-and-green, evergreen-bough-bedecked, fake-snow-sprinkled winter wonderland, I realized that with everything going on, I'd nearly forgotten how quickly Christmas was approaching. I did some quick mental math and realized it was just over a week away, and I had virtually nothing done to prepare. If I didn't get this murder figured out soon, all Matt would find under the tree on Christmas morning was one of Latte's drooled-on chew toys. At least I'd be setting the expectation low for future Christmases.

The school's doors had just opened to let the playgoers in when I saw Mike slip in among the crowd. I felt my stomach clench. He couldn't possibly have found out I went to see Brett in the hospital, could he? I didn't see how. I told myself he was just there to help with security and busied myself with serving people snacks. I was successful until the lights flashed, letting everyone know the play was about to start, and the lobby cleared. Then Mike walked over to our table.

"Sammy, could you give us a minute?" he asked.

"Sure," she said, wiping her hands on her apron. She shot me a sympathetic look and headed toward the bathroom.

"What's up?" I asked as cheerfully as I could.

"I think you know," he said coldly.

I swallowed hard.

"You went to see Brett in the hospital."

"Um, what did—how did—" I stammered and stuttered and couldn't get my words out.

"His mother wants to press charges."

"What? For what?"

"Harassment. You've repeatedly met with or attempted to meet with Brett while insinuating that he was responsible for or involved in Veronica Underwood's murder."

"But Brett asked me to go visit him!"

"Brett is a juvenile."

"Mike, you can't possibly think that I had any malicious intent!"

He shook his head slowly, but I saw no sympathy in the gesture. "I told you to stay away."

I stared at him for what felt like a very long time. Finally, I managed to put the question thundering around my head into words. "Are you arresting me?"

"Not now," he said, sending a jolt of anxiety through my system. "But after the play, I'm going to need you to come down to the station with me so I can take your statement."

"Will I be going home tonight?" I asked.

"Because if not, I'll need to make arrangements for my dog."

"That shouldn't be necessary," he said. "As long as you cooperate."

I nodded briefly. I could cooperate. I might think it was ridiculous, but I could cooperate.

"I'll see you after the play," Mike said then turned on his heel and walked away toward the other side of the large, open area we were set up in. He leaned up against the wall, where I guessed he was planning to stay for the rest of the show.

We were friends, I thought, staring over at him. I didn't really understand what had happened. Sure, I'd gotten involved in his investigation and hadn't stepped away from it when he'd asked me to, but I'd done all that before. Maybe he'd just had enough of it. Maybe everything with Brett had really upset him that much. I could understand that. But his reaction seemed so extreme, so disproportionate. But maybe I was wrong. Maybe I'd taken advantage of our friendship, assumed I could get away with things that I shouldn't have. I still held out a fragile hope that maybe our friendship wasn't gone for good, but I wasn't terribly optimistic.

"What was that about?" Sammy asked, coming up behind me.

"Nothing," I said. "It was nothing." I suddenly

felt overwhelmed. I had lost a friend, was facing harassment charges, hadn't done a thing to prepare for Christmas, and for what? What did I have to show for it? Nothing. Not a solved case, not a vindicated teacher. I had not a single thing to show for it. "Did we bring a knife?" I asked Sammy, looking for a reason to get away for a few minutes. "I need a knife to cut the cinnamon loaf so we have some ready for intermission. I'll go look for one in the kitchen." I turned to go toward the cafeteria, even as I heard Sammy saying behind me that she had one right there. I just needed to be alone. Just for a minute.

I made my way down the hallway and through the doors into the darkened cafeteria. There was a light on in the kitchen. I followed it, knowing I'd need to return with a knife to maintain my cover story. I had just gotten into the kitchen when I heard voices.

"Why did you have a folder anyway, Marcus?" a female voice asked. "And why did you just leave it out on your desk where anyone could see it?"

"Because I didn't expect anyone to be going through my papers, Gwen!"

Marcus. Gwen. Marcus Varros and Gwen Blarney. And were they—could they possibly be talking about the papers that Brett had stolen? The ones he'd taken the pictures of? I ducked down and crept closer to them.

"Not even Brett Wallace? Are you an idiot, Marcus? You know that boy can't be left alone for two seconds without getting into something!"

"Well, if you didn't send him to my office every day, it wouldn't be such a problem. You can't even control your classroom!"

"Maybe if you hadn't dumped me in the English department, I wouldn't be having trouble with it! You know I've never been a good English teacher! It bores me! But no, your little girlfriend comes running, asking for a job, and you just shove me aside and give my job to her!"

"Veronica wasn't my girlfriend, and you know it! Besides, she was going to tell my wife about us."

"About the two of us? Or about the two of you?"

"I told you, Gwen! We weren't together!"

"Then why did I catch you kissing her?"

"I told you. It was a one-time thing! It meant nothing."

"I've heard that before. Your lies don't work on me, Marcus. Not when you tell your wife the same ones when you're talking about me!" Gwen's heels started clip-clopping in my direction. I scooted back a little farther to stay hidden.

"Stop it, Gwen! You know you're not just some fling. I love you! I'd do anything for you. I'd die for you! I'd—I'd—" Varros's footsteps followed her toward me. I shrank back some more.

"You'd kill for me?"

"You know I would."

"Say it." Gwen's voice was lower now. I could just barely hear it. Varros must have been standing very close to her.

"I would kill for you." He paused. "I killed for you."

The talking stopped, but I heard noises I couldn't quite recognize. On my hands and knees, I crept toward them, trying to see what was going on without being seen myself. Unfortunately, I failed to take into account the need to also not be heard and bumped into a cart piled high with metal pots that came crashing down onto the tile floor.

"What was that?" Gwen asked.

"Someone's here."

I tried to scramble to my feet but kept getting tripped up on the pots. Finally, I managed to get myself up.

"Just where do you think you're going?" Varros asked from behind me.

"Oh, I was just looking for a knife to cut the cinnamon loaf, but it looks like I'm interrupting, so

I'll just be on my way." I said it all without turning around and started to make for the door.

"Then you're in luck. I have a knife right here for you."

"Oh, thank you!" I turned around, naively assuming he was actually about to give me a knife. He was—he just had no intention of putting it into my hand. More like my chest.

Varros brandished one of the biggest butcher knives I'd ever seen in my direction. "Thought you could just sneak in here to get some evidence for your little investigation, huh? Because Ann Crowsdale's *so nice* she just can't go to jail! You're probably going to run straight to the cops and tell them everything, aren't you?"

Gwen stepped up and grabbed Varros's arm. "Marcus, stop. She may not have heard anything."

"Oh, she heard everything. Didn't you, Fran?"

I tried to swallow, but my mouth was dry. "No, not really," I squeaked.

"You're a terrible liar." He stepped away from Gwen and toward me, still pointing the knife decidedly in my direction. "You wanted to hear me swear I'd kill for you, Gwen?" he asked. "Killing Veronica wasn't enough for you? I'll prove how much I love you. And this time you can watch."

I tried to look around the room for something I

could use to defend myself while not taking my eyes off Varros. I knew that looking away for a split second would be all he needed to reach me with the knife. If he even needed that.

"Marcus, I don't—I don't want to see her die!"

"You always were a coward, Gwen." He stepped closer to me. I stepped back, straight into the wall. There was nowhere to go. "It's just too bad Ann's out there watching the play," Varros said. "I'll just have to pin this one on you."

He made a move toward me, and I squeezed my eyes shut. If I only had a second left to live, I wanted the last image in my head to be of my Matty and Latte, not this monster.

"Freeze!"

It seemed like a strange thing for someone to say right before they murdered you, but I wasn't planning on moving anyway, so I complied.

"Drop the weapon, and put your hands in the air!"

I didn't have a weapon, so I just slowly raised my hands into the air above my head.

"Not you, Franny."

And that was when I realized the voice wasn't coming from Varros. I slowly opened my eyes. I'd never been so happy to see Mike in my life. Even if he was pointing a gun in my general direction.

"Get down on your knees, both of you," he barked.

I started to get down, when I realized he was talking to Gwen and Varros. They got down. I stayed put.

"Franny, go out in the hall and wait for the other officers. When they get here, show them where to go. They should be here any minute."

"Will you be okay here?" I asked. "Alone? With them?"

"I'll be more okay than you were."

I almost burst into tears when he smiled at me. Maybe I hadn't lost my friend after all.

Chapter 25

"FRANNY, I AM SO SORRY."

"You don't have to keep telling me that, Mike. It's fine!"

A week had gone by since the play's opening night when Mike had stopped Varros from killing me, and he was still apologizing for everything that had happened.

"No, but really, Fran. I never should have been so hard on you."

"Stop it! I don't want to hear another word about it out of you. Now where are Sandra and the kids? Why aren't they here?"

"They're already up at her parents' cabin. I'll head up tomorrow morning after I get off duty."

"How did you get stuck working Christmas Eve,

anyway? Aren't you high-ranking enough that you shouldn't have to work major holidays?"

He shrugged. "Somebody's gotta do it."

I looked across the café at Ryan, cuddled up in the corner with Sammy, noticeably not in his uniform, unlike Mike. As he was ostensibly the low man on the police department's totem pole, having only started working in Cape Bay less than four months earlier, I didn't understand why he wasn't the one spending Christmas Eve patrolling Cape Bay's sleepy streets, but I wasn't the one who made the schedule, so what did I know?

"Well, I'm glad you're here, anyway." I slipped my arm around his waist and gave him a sideways hug. "And I'm glad you're not yelling at me anymore."

He laughed. "Me too, Franny."

I spotted Rhonda waving at me across the crowded room. "The kid-friendly eggnog is the one on the left," I told him as I excused myself. Since he was working, he had to skip the rum-soaked stuff. I wasn't complaining, though. It was more for me.

I made my way through all the friends and friends-of-friends who had gathered at the café for our first annual Christmas party. I'd thought about having it at my house, but I'd never managed to get it very decorated. Sammy, though, had the café completely transformed, even above and beyond how she'd had it for the rest of the season. Just about everywhere I looked had something special and Christmassy. It was so festive. I was going to be sad when we had to take it all down.

I finally got to Rhonda after saying hello and Merry Christmas and giving hugs to about twenty people.

"You should have brought Mike over with you!" she said loudly so I could hear her over all the Christmas music and conversation.

I looked across the room at him standing all alone at the punch bowl. "He does look lonely, doesn't he?"

"Well, yeah, but I meant because I still haven't heard the details of how the whole Underwood thing went down, and I figure you've been hitting the eggnog too hard for too long to remember it all!"

"I most certainly have not!"

"All right, then! Spill! I know Varros is the one who killed Veronica Underwood, and she was blackmailing him about something or other, but I'm missing all the details."

I started from as near as possible to what I knew as the beginning. "So Varros and his wife used to live in Rhode Island, right? He and Veronica and her friend Kristin all apparently knew each other for a really long time. At some point, maybe before Varros got married, maybe after—the details aren't too clear—he and Veronica got together."

"He was cheating on his wife with her."

"Yup. And apparently Veronica wanted to be a teacher even though she quite openly hated children. I guess she thought it would be an easy job or something. Anyway, she didn't want to go through all the work to become a teacher, so she falsified her records to get her teaching certificate."

"And Varros helped her, right?"

"They think so. They're not totally sure. He definitely knew they were fake, but they haven't figured out whether he helped her fake them. So they were together back in Rhode Island, but then Varros and his wife decided to move here. I'm not too clear on the details of that either, but I think she had some family here she wanted to be closer to or something like that."

"You're not too clear on many of the details are you?" Rhonda teased.

"I know the important ones! Anyway, once they were here and Varros started working at Cape Bay High, he and Gwen Blarney got together."

"Still cheating, right?"

"Still cheating. He and Mrs. Varros are still

together. Well, they were. I heard she's filed for divorce already."

"Can't say I blame her!" Rhonda said.

"Me neither. Anyway, Veronica found out that the Rhode Island Department of Education was onto her fake credentials, so she contacted Varros and told him she needed a job here. If he didn't give it to her, she was going to spill the beans to his wife about the two of them."

"Were they still together?"

"Apparently, yes."

"So he was cheating with Gwen Blarney and Veronica Underwood at the same time."

"Yup. And Veronica knew about Gwen too. She just used it to blackmail him more. He eventually got sick of her always asking for money and threatening to out him to his wife, so he killed her."

Rhonda shivered visibly despite the heat of the room.

"What I think is so creepy about it is how methodical he was. He disabled the camera that covered the part of the parking lot where her assigned spot was and made sure everyone in the school knew it was broken. He slashed her tires to keep her there late after play practice when he knew that she and Ann Crowsdale would be the last two leaving. He knew that Veronica didn't carry a tire iron but that Ann did because he'd had a flat tire the year before and she'd let him borrow it."

"So he knew she'd let Veronica borrow it and then her fingerprints would be on it."

I nodded. "He had everything planned down to a T. He knew everyone's schedules and made his plan so that if Ann Crowsdale fell through, there would be plenty of other people to pin it on, including his other girlfriend, Gwen."

Rhonda shook her head. "So what did he have against Ann that he wanted to set her up for murder?"

"Absolutely nothing. She was just the easiest target."

"Of course, if he'd picked someone less well loved to pin it on, the truth may not have ever come out."

"The biggest flaw in his plan," I agreed.

"What about Brett? How was he involved?"

"He wasn't. Except for the evidence he found that was enough to prove Varros's motive."

"I told you the kid's a genius." Rhonda smiled.

"Oh, trust me, I believe you."

"I'm going to go get some more eggnog. Do you want more?" Rhonda asked me.

I looked at my still half-full cup. "Nope, I think I'm good."

Rhonda headed for the punch bowls, and I wandered over to the corner where Ryan and Sammy were sitting. Sammy's best friend, Dawn, had joined them, so I didn't feel as if I was interrupting. We sat and talked for a few minutes before the conversation turned to Sammy and Ryan's plans to drive up to Plymouth after the party to celebrate Christmas with Ryan's family.

"So how did you get out of working Christmas Eve, anyhow?" I asked him.

He shrugged. "Just lucky, I guess."

"It just seems weird that Mike got stuck working when he's been there for so long."

"He's working the twenty-sixth too. First shift. He's supposed to drive back tomorrow night."

"What? That's ridiculous! He has kids."

"I dunno," Ryan said. "I heard he volunteered."

I made a face. That didn't sound right. He'd barely have any time with Sandra and the kids. I suspected there was something more going on in the department that Ryan didn't know about or wasn't privy to since he was so new. I hoped so, anyway.

"Anybody want more eggnog?" Ryan asked. Sammy and Dawn both passed him their cups. I hadn't made much more of a dent in mine.

"I better go refill the bowls," Sammy said. "It

looks like they're getting low." She got up and headed for the back room to get some of the pitchers of eggnog we'd prefilled.

I sat and talked to Dawn for a few minutes before someone came and asked me if there were any more napkins. "I'll go get them," I said and excused myself.

I walked in the back room and found Sammy standing there, staring at her phone.

"Everything okay?" I asked.

She held her phone out for me to see what was on the screen. It was a text message from a local number that she didn't have saved.

Hope you and Ry-Ry have a very merry Christmas up here in Plymouth. His mom makes the BEST mashed pota-toes. Tell her I said hi! Love, Cheryl

"You've been texting Cheryl?" I asked. Sammy was a turn-the-other-cheek kind of girl, but that seemed a bit much, even for her.

She shook her head. "No, she just texts me." Still holding the phone so I could see, she began to scroll up. And up. And up. There were dozens of texts from Cheryl and no replies from Sammy.

"How long has this been going on?"

She shrugged. "A little over a week. Since that day you called the police on her and her friends."

"But, Sammy, there are dozens!" In just a week?

265

"I know." She slid the phone into her pocket. "She sends them all day long."

"Have you told Ryan?"

"No. And I'm not going to. I don't want to upset him."

"Sammy, I think he'd want to know."

"No." She shook her head adamantly. "I'm not telling him, and you're not going to tell him either."

I didn't want to, but eventually I nodded. "All right. For now. But if she keeps this up, we're going to have another talk about it, okay?"

She nodded. "Thanks, Fran."

"There you are!" Ryan said, poking his head in the room. "I've been looking all over for you!"

"And you found me."

"I have more eggnog for you."

"And I have more for the bowl," she said, holding up one of the pitchers.

"We could always just drink out of that," Ryan joked.

My heart felt a little sick as I heard Sammy's pretty laugh. Ryan had no idea what she was going through.

"*Ciao, bella!*"

I smiled as Matt walked into the storage room. He smiled back, but then his faded. "What's wrong?" he asked, exercising his unnatural ability to read my moods.

I shrugged. "Just a rough couple of weeks, I guess. And, you know, my mom."

"I know," he said. "I feel the same way." He pulled me into a hug.

It was the first Christmas since my mom and his dad had died. It was hard for both of us, but it helped that we each knew what the other was going through. And that we had each other. I didn't know what I'd have done if I hadn't had Matt to lean on, sometimes literally.

"Should we go back out to the party?" he asked after a minute.

"Mm-hmm," I murmured against his chest. I indulged in the feeling of his body against mine for another minute and then pulled away. "Let's go."

"After you, *bella*," he said, gesturing for me to go first.

I was out the door and he was halfway when he grabbed my arm and pulled me back. "Not so fast," he said. I was confused until he pointed up at the mistletoe hanging in the doorway above our heads. "Merry Christmas, Franny," he whispered as he pulled me into him.

I smiled as he leaned down to kiss me. "Merry Christmas, Matty."

Recipe 1: Café Crema

Ingredients:

- Arabica beans

Café cremas are 6 to 8 oz of coffee brewed using an espresso machine. For a good cup of crema, use a coarser grind of the bean to slow down the extraction (20 to 30 seconds). The drink should have a nice layer of crema on top of the coffee, and not too watery.

Recipe 2: Gingerbread Cookies

Makes 24

Ingredients:

- 3 cups all-purpose flour
- 1 large egg
- 1 ½ tsp baking powder
- ½ cup molasses
- ¾ tsp baking soda
- ¼ tsp salt
- 1 tbsp ground ginger
- 2 tsp vanilla
- 1 ¾ tsp ground cinnamon
- ¼ tsp ground cloves
- 6 tbsp unsalted butter

- ¾ cup dark brown sugar

Whisk flour, baking powder, baking soda, salt, ginger, cinnamon, and cloves in a small bowl until well blended.

In another bowl, beat butter, brown sugar, and egg on medium speed until well blended. Add molasses and vanilla and mix again. Pour in dry ingredients and blend smooth.

Divide dough in half. Wrap each in plastic and let stand at room temperature from 2 to 8 hours.

Roll out dough over a floured surface until ¼-inch thick. Use more flour as needed to avoid sticking. Cut cookies with gingerbread man cutter or your desired shape.

Using baking sheets lined with greased parchment paper, bake at 375° F for 7 to 10 minutes. After they cool, you can use colored frosting to decorate them.

Recipe 3: Sugar Cookies

Makes up to 5 dozen

Ingredients:
- 5 cups all-purpose flour
- 4 eggs
- 2 cups sugar
- 1 ½ cups butter, softened
- 2 tsp baking powder
- 1 tsp salt
- 1 tsp vanilla extract

Beat butter and sugar in a bowl until smooth. Beat in eggs and vanilla. Then, stir in flour, baking powder, and salt. Cover. Chill dough for 1 hour to overnight.

Roll out dough on floured surface to $\frac{1}{4}$-inch thickness. Cut into your desired shapes, Christmas-themed or otherwise. Bake at 400° F for 6 to 8 minutes. Let cool completely and you have the option of using colored frosting to decorate them.

About the Author

Harper Lin is the *USA TODAY* bestselling author of 6 cozy mystery series including *The Patisserie Mysteries* and *The Cape Bay Cafe Mysteries*.

When she's not reading or writing mysteries, she loves going to yoga classes, hiking, and hanging out with her family and friends.

www.HarperLin.com

54616020R00171

Made in the USA
San Bernardino, CA
21 October 2017